CaLiFORNiA SCHEMiNG

<u>"Saved by the Bell" titles include:</u>

Mark-Paul Gosselaar: Ultimate Gold

Mario Lopez: High-Voltage Star

Behind the Scenes at "Saved by the Bell"

Beauty and Fitness with "Saved by the Bell"

▲   ▼   ▲

<u>*Hot new fiction titles:*</u>

Zack Strikes Back

Bayside Madness

California Scheming

Girls' Night Out

Zack's Last Scam

Class Trip Chaos

CALIFORNIA SCHEMING

by Beth Cruise

Collier Books
Macmillan Publishing Company
New York
Maxwell Macmillan Canada
Toronto
Maxwell Macmillan International
New York   Oxford   Singapore   Sydney

Collier Books
Macmillan Publishing Company
866 Third Avenue
New York, NY 10022

Maxwell Macmillan Canada, Inc.
1200 Eglinton Avenue East
Suite 200
Don Mills, Ontario M3C 3N1

Macmillan Publishing Company is part of the Maxwell
Communication Group of Companies.

First Collier Books edition 1992
Printed in the United States of America
10 9 8 7 6 5 4 3 2

Library of Congress Cataloging-in-Publication Data
Cruise, Beth.
California scheming / by Beth Cruise. — 1st Collier Books ed.
        p.   cm.
Summary: The "Saved by the Bell" gang spends spring break in San
Francisco when Lisa wins a design contest and is invited to attend a
well-known designer's fashion show.
ISBN 0-02-042776-X
[1. Fashion—Fiction.   2. San Francisco (Calif.)—Fiction.]
        I. Title.
PZ7.C88827Cal   1992
[Fic]—dc20   92-2739

**To the
"Saved by the Bell"
crew**

CaLiFORNiA
SCHEMiNG

Chapter 1

When the final bell rang on Friday afternoon at Bayside High, the school exploded in pandemonium. Kids ran through the halls shouting, and someone wrapped the huge victory banner from the previous week's football game around the cheerleaders, tied a bow in the front, and left them squealing in the downstairs hall. The principal, Mr. Belding, didn't even try to calm everyone down. He just went into his office and locked the door.

Zack Morris stood with his arms crossed in the middle of the hallway, looking around with satisfaction at the chaos. "At last," he said with a happy sigh. "Now, this is the way school *should* be."

He turned back to his friends. "So what is causing this strange outbreak? Two little words. Take them separately, and what do you have?"

Zack held up one hand. "The first word: a season with no football." He held up the other hand. "The second? Bad luck on a ski trip. But put the two words together—" Zack clapped his hands, his hazel eyes twinkling. "And you get swept away into fantasyland—spring break!"

"Whew," Samuel Powers said, shaking his frizzy curls. "I thought you were going to say summer avalanche. Now, *that's* a way to get swept away."

Samuel was better known as Screech, and he deserved the zany nickname. The electric curls and skinny body encased in a very strange wardrobe only concealed an even more eccentric mind. Screech's logic was like an out-of-control train. It had amazing speed and no regard for direction.

A. C. Slater slung a muscled arm around Screech's slight shoulders, nearly sending him to the floor. "That's why we're taking up a collection for you, Screech," he told him. "We're sending you to the Alps for the summer."

"Gee, I'd better dust off my lederhosen," Screech said thoughtfully.

Jessie Spano grinned as she gently removed Slater's arm, letting Screech straighten up. She nestled closer to Slater and swept a lock of long, curly brown hair behind her shoulder. Jessie and Slater had dated and split up more times than anyone could count, but at that moment, they were breaking their own record. They hadn't had a fight since nine that morning.

"So what are your plans, Zack?" Jessie asked. "You always have a scheme cooking for spring break."

Zack sighed and ran a hand through his blond hair. "That's just the trouble," he said. "Starting tomorrow, it looks like I'll be spending ten days at the beach."

"That sounds awful," Jessie teased, her light hazel eyes sparkling.

"It is," Zack insisted. "It's what I do every weekend. Spring break should be exciting. It should offer new worlds to conquer."

"Well, I'll be conquering the frozen yogurt machine at the mall," Kelly Kapowski said regretfully. Her deep blue eyes were rueful, and she hugged her books to her chest. "I need to make money for my college fund. I'd give anything to be able to just hang out at the beach."

"I wish you could, too, Kelly," Zack said sympathetically. He meant it. The beach just wouldn't be the same without the fantastic sight of Kelly in a bikini. Boredom was impossible when Kelly's gorgeous bod was around. But Zack mentally closed his eyes against Kelly's image. He'd already blown it with his ex-girlfriend. Zack Morris might be in her future, but not anytime soon. Kelly had made that painfully clear just a short time ago.

Slater must have caught his brain wave. "I don't mind the beach, either," he remarked with a glance at Jessie. "Especially if you get a new bikini, momma." His deep dimples flashed as he gave her a devilish grin.

Jessie poked him playfully. "I agree with Zack," she said. "We have to think of something special to do. I've already planned to tackle three books on my reading list, but that's the only fun I'm looking forward to."

Zack rolled his eyes. He'd been best friends with Jessie since kindergarten, but he still couldn't figure out why someone with such a gorgeous head would want to fill it with academics. Even the influence of easygoing Slater hadn't changed Jessie's passionate interests in school, women's rights, and baby seals, not to mention her campaign to get the cheerleaders to quit and try out for the football team—as soon as someone untied them.

"Don't worry, Jessie," he told her. "As the premier schemer of Bayside High, I guarantee I'll come up with a plan to make our spring break memorable."

"I don't know why you guys are all so worried about spring break," Screech put in. "The probability of having a perfect time is pretty low."

"Hey, what's with all this doom and gloom, Screech?" Zack asked.

"He's been like this all week," Kelly said.

"I'm doing a project for Mr. Sandusky on probability," Screech informed them. "You'd be surprised what a thread we're all hanging from, Zack. Do you know that you have a one-in-six-thousand chance of being hit by a falling asteroid?"

"Are you sure you haven't been hit by one already, Screech?" Jessie asked.

"I wonder what Lisa is doing for spring break," Kelly said, getting back to the subject. "Maybe she has a fun plan."

Zack snorted. "Sure, Kelly. If we want to spend our break checking out sales at the mall, Lisa is the perfect person to consult."

"That's not fair," Kelly said, defending her friend. "Lisa is interested in other things, too."

"Sure," Slater agreed. "She doesn't just think about clothes. She thinks about makeup, too."

Zack and Slater guffawed, and Jessie and Kelly couldn't help grinning. As much as they adored Lisa Turtle, their best friend, even they had to admit she was obsessed with fashion. Of course, the gorgeous black teen was also crazy about boys—when she could fit them in between trips to the mall.

Just then, Lisa ran down the hall and skidded to a stop in front of them. She gave a little excited jump, then another. "Guess what!" she panted. "Guess, guess, guess!"

"You found the perfect shade of nail polish to

match your new lipstick?'' Jessie asked.

Lisa shook her head, her soft brown eyes sparkling.

"Your father gave you his credit card for a shopping spree?'' Kelly teased.

"You found a faster route to the mall?'' Zack tried.

"The asteroid missed you by inches?'' Screech squeaked.

Lisa shook her head. "I won the California Young Designer to Watch Contest!'' she squealed.

"The what?'' Slater asked.

"You designed a watch?'' Screech asked, scratching his head.

"A suit,'' Lisa told them. "Remember when I drove you all crazy designing those outfits last summer?''

"How could we forget?'' Zack groaned. "I let you pin yellow chiffon on me. I couldn't face the guys at the beach for weeks.''

"Well, my entry won!'' Lisa enthused. "I just called home, and my mom told me. I'm so excited!''

"What's the prize?'' Jessie asked.

"If it's money, I want you to know I'm available to help spend it,'' Zack advised with a winning smile. "I'm even free for dinner tonight.''

"Dream on,'' Lisa said. "I don't get money, anyway. I get something better. A photography shoot with Isidore Duncan!''

Kelly and Jessie squealed, but Zack, Slater, and Screech looked at each other with puzzled expressions. "Who?" Zack asked.

"Isidore Duncan is the hottest designer in California," Kelly told them. "His clothes are fantastic."

"He's flying down from San Francisco tomorrow and a famous photographer is going to take our picture," Lisa said. "There'll be one model wearing my design in the photograph, and one model will wear one of his. It's going to be in the Sunday supplement in the Palisades *Gazette*! And guess who's going to shoot it—Niles Madrid."

"Wow," Kelly breathed. "He's a really famous photographer. All the models want to work with him."

"That's fantastic, Lisa," Jessie enthused.

"We're so proud of you," Kelly said.

Slater nodded. "Good stuff, Lisa."

"Maybe you could get me a deal on a new leather jacket," Zack said thoughtfully. "My old one is looking kind of shabby."

Screech sighed. "I just hope this success won't take you away from us, Lisa. But I'll wait for you, no matter what." Screech had had a crush on Lisa since they were kids.

"Wait, there's more," Lisa went on, ignoring Screech the way she usually did. "Isidore was so impressed with my design that he sent a letter inviting me to be his personal guest at his fashion show in San Francisco next week! He said he wants to include the outfit I designed in the show. Can you believe it?"

"Wow," Kelly said. "That's such an honor."

"It's incredible," Jessie agreed.

"Not so incredible," Lisa said, her smile turning into a frown. "My parents won't foot the bill for the trip. Hotels are really expensive, and besides, they can't take the time off from work. And there's no way they'd let me go alone." Lisa's parents were both doctors, and they were superdedicated.

"That's too bad," Slater sympathized. "Parents will pull that kind of stuff, though."

"At least you get to go on the fashion shoot," Jessie said.

"With Niles Madrid," Kelly put in.

Lisa nodded. "I know. But imagine being invited to Isidore Duncan's fashion show! I can't believe I have stay home. And it's so perfect—it's during spring break. I wouldn't even have to miss school."

"You're just going to have to hang out at the beach with us, Lisa," Zack said.

"Don't worry, Lisa, you still have me," Screech said, putting a hand on her shoulder.

"That's my problem," Lisa groaned, removing his hand with the tips of her fingers.

"Well, it looks like spring break is a bust this year for all of us," Zack said philosophically. "Let's hit the Max and drown our sorrows in a couple of shots of root beer."

They all headed for the exit. Jessie followed behind the rest of the gang, frowning in thought. An idea had floated into her brain, and she needed time to think about it. It must be Zack's influence, because the idea was pretty crazy and she didn't know if she could pull it off. But if she did, it might be the greatest spring break ever!

▲   ▼   ▲

Later that afternoon at the Max, the gang was nursing their third round of sodas along with the sweet taste of freedom. The only one who wasn't excited by the prospect of ten whole days off was Screech.

"I don't know why you all aren't more worried," he said to the gang. "The sun has a higher probability of going into nova than you think."

Lisa sighed. "If you don't stop with all this probability junk, I'm going to get *into* a Nova and drive over your skinny body."

"Screech, you've got to lighten up," Zack advised. "You can't keep thinking about all this stuff."

"Life is wonderful, Screech," Kelly said. "Look at Lisa. She just won a fabulous contest. Isn't that great?"

"Sure, but she doesn't get to go to San Francisco, does she?" Screech pointed out.

"Speaking of that, I might have some news . . . ," Jessie started, but her voice trailed off when everyone looked at her.

"What?" Lisa asked.

"You sure were on the phone for a while," Kelly said. "Who did you call?"

"Come on, Jess," Zack said. "Out with it."

Jessie pushed her soda away. "Well," she admitted, her hazel eyes shining. "I didn't want to say anything until I knew for sure. But it looks like I found a way to get Lisa to San Francisco!"

"What are you talking about, Jessie?" Lisa asked doubtfully. "My parents would never let me go alone."

"But what if you went with all of us?" Jessie asked slyly. "And had a chaperone up in San Francisco? A responsible parent—my father."

"Your father?" Kelly said. "That's right. He lives in San Francisco."

Lisa gasped. "You'd better spell this out, girl, because I am about to get totally excited."

"Okay," Jessie said with a grin. "I just called my father and told him about your problem. And he said he's sure he can line up two free rooms for us in the King Cole Hotel for five whole days!" Jessie's father was an executive in a hotel chain, and one of its flagship hotels was the world-famous King Cole.

"Oh, my gosh!" Lisa squealed, standing up half-way. "This is fantastic!"

"You'd have to share a room with me and Kelly, though," Jessie said.

"I'd share a room with Godzilla if I got to go to San Francisco," Lisa breathed. "I'd even share a room with Screech. Well," she amended, as Screech sat up brightly, "I wouldn't go that far."

"And Slater, Zack, and Screech can share a room," Jessie went on. "It's perfect."

"Jessie, I must admit you really pulled this one off," Zack said admiringly. "Spring break is sure looking up."

"It's incredible," Slater agreed, slinging an arm around Jessie. "Way to go."

Screech frowned thoughtfully. "I'm going to have to look up some earthquake statistics."

"Okay, now I *am* totally excited," Lisa breathed happily.

Then Kelly spoke up in a small voice. "Gee," she said, "Have a wonderful time, you guys."

Chapter 2

Everyone stopped in their tracks. They all looked at Kelly, whose deep blue eyes were filling with tears.

"Gosh, Kelly," Lisa said. "I forgot all about your job."

"You can't afford to go?" Jessie asked.

Kelly's silky hair flew as she shook her head. "A free room from your dad is great," she told Jessie. "But there's still meals and stuff. Not to mention airfare. And I really needed this time to make money for school next year."

Everyone slumped down in their chairs. Kelly came from a large family. They had plenty of love but not much cash. She was always having to get various after-school jobs to earn money for clothes and college.

"Well, if you can't go, none of us will go," Lisa said stoutly.

"Lisa, don't be silly," Kelly said, dabbing her eyes with a napkin. "You guys *have* to go. I'd only feel worse if you stayed home because of me."

"But we wouldn't have any fun without you," Jessie protested.

"I wouldn't go that far," Slater said, but Jessie elbowed him. "Oof," he said. "I mean, of course we wouldn't have any fun," he amended quickly.

"Thanks, you guys," Kelly said sadly. "That's really sweet. But we all know that Lisa can't miss this opportunity. You've just got to go to San Francisco."

It's just like Kelly to be unselfish, Zack thought, *but Lisa and Jessie are right—it won't be the same without her. And this is my chance to have five whole days with Kelly away from all the usual distractions of school, homework, cheerleading practice—and other guys. I could make some serious progress in foggy, romantic San Francisco.*

Zack had to find a way to get her on the trip! What he needed was a plan—and fast.

▲   ▼   ▲

The next morning, Lisa was a nervous wreck. It was the day of the big shoot, and she was sure she'd wear the absolute wrong thing. She tore off her fourth outfit of the morning and slipped on the hot pink jacket and purple skirt she'd designed herself. It had been the first thing she'd tried on that morning, but it just hadn't looked right. Absolutely nothing in her closet had looked right, though, and next to the outfit that had won the contest, this was her favorite. It had a row of different-colored big gems as buttons, and when she added a cute hat that matched the skirt, she had to admit that she didn't look as terrible as she'd thought earlier. Anyway, she didn't have time to change again.

Lisa hurried down the stairs and into the kitchen, where she thought she'd left her purse and car keys. They were nowhere to be found. "Mom?" she called. "Have you seen my keys?"

"No, honey," her mother called back. "Have you misplaced them?"

"Oh, gosh," Lisa moaned, dashing out of the kitchen toward the living room. "I can't believe it! I'm going to be late!"

"Relax, sweetie," Dr. Turtle urged, following her into the living room. She was a neat, impeccably organized woman who was sometimes at a loss how to cope with her unpredictable daughter. "You can borrow my car."

"But my purse!" Lisa wailed. "It has my makeup in it!"

"I'm sure they'll have makeup at the photography studio," her mother pointed out calmly.

"And my driver's license," Lisa went on, throwing the pillows on the couch into the air as she searched for her purse.

"That's something you'll definitely need," her mother agreed as she scanned the room for the purse.

"I'll never make it," Lisa said, squirming underneath the couch to look for her purse. Just then, there was a knock at the front door.

"If you have my purse, come in!" Lisa cried in a hysterical voice.

Dr. Turtle shook her head. "Honestly, Lisa," she said, amusement bubbling in her voice. "This isn't the end of the world, you know."

"You'd be surprised, Dr. Turtle," Screech said as he entered the living room. "The earth could be hurtling into the sun even as we speak."

Zack came in behind Screech, carrying a black leather pouch. "I found this by the front door," he said.

"My purse!" Lisa cried, springing toward it.

"We came to see if you needed a ride to the shoot," Zack explained, handing the purse to Lisa. *And to follow through on my plan*, he added to himself.

"I think that's an excellent idea," Lisa's mother said. "I'm afraid Lisa would drive straight into a tree today."

"Thanks, you guys," Lisa breathed. "Can we go right this minute? I can't be late."

"My chariot awaits," Zack said with a dramatic gesture.

"And don't worry," Screech said. "Our chances of getting in an accident on the way are probably no more than one in thirty. Maybe twenty-five, tops."

"Screech, your chances of making it through the morning aren't very good at all," Lisa said grimly.

"Good luck, sweetie," Dr. Turtle said, giving Lisa a quick kiss. "You'll be great. And you look absolutely gorgeous."

"Now, that's something I'd always bet on," Screech said with a satisfied nod.

Lisa took off her hat and swatted him with it.

"What did you do that for?" Screech asked, aggrieved.

"It's even more aggravating when you say something reasonably human," Lisa grumbled as she swept out the door.

▲   ▼   ▲

Niles Madrid's studio was in a gleaming industrial building on the edge of town, right by the beach. "Wow," Zack said approvingly as he eased his Mustang into a parking spot. "What a cool building."

"It is a cool place," Lisa agreed, her teeth chattering. "Too cool for me. I feel like a dweeb. They're going to be able to tell, too. As soon as I walk in the door, Niles will look at Isidore and they'll say, 'Who's the dweeb?' "

"Don't worry, Lisa," Screech said manfully. "I'll walk in first."

Lisa gave him a dry look. "That's really reassuring, Screech."

They climbed out of the car and started toward the door of the building. Screech and Lisa went in, with Zack bringing up the rear. Just as he started in, he almost bumped into a tall, slim girl carrying a makeup case. He noticed that the girl had gorgeous, thick blond hair to the middle of her back and wide-set green eyes. Zack instantly guessed that she was one of the models. *This is going to be a cinch*, he thought. *It fits in perfectly with my plan.*

"Excuse me," Zack said, stepping back and holding the door.

"Sorry," the girl said. "I'm kind of late."

He gave her his most engaging grin. "Then I don't want to hold you up. You must be here for the Duncan shoot."

She nodded. "I just got called the other day. Too bad I'm not wearing his clothes, though. I have to wear some high school student's design." She sniffed. "I just hope it's not a T-shirt and gym socks."

"I hope so, too," Zack said sincerely.

"I'm Shana," she told him as they entered the studio.

"Zack. I'm really glad to meet you, Shana."

"Do you work with Niles?" Shana asked, swinging her thick golden hair behind one thin shoulder.

Zack shrugged. "Here and there, there and here—you know how it is," he said vaguely.

"Sure," she said, nodding. "Totally."

Across the huge, bright studio, Niles Madrid was fussing with lights and snapping at his assistant. "I said *diffused*," he yelled fiercely, and then lowered his voice and continued in an inaudible tone.

A slender, cute guy with curly black hair stood watching Niles, a slight smile curving his lips. He was dressed in jeans, a white T-shirt, and a baseball cap, and he looked like the only assistant who wasn't afraid of the photographer. He chugged at an orange juice carton and checked his watch.

"Who's that?" Zack asked the model.

She gave him a surprised look. "It's Isidore Duncan," she said. "Don't you recognize him?"

"Oh, of course," Zack said quickly. "I didn't recognize him with the cap on. He looks younger."

"Wow," Lisa breathed, suddenly appearing at Zack's side. "He's so cute."

Zack started to reply, but Lisa had already started to move off, a dazed look on her face.

Screech headed for the refreshments set up on a long table near a small kitchen.

Zack turned to Shana. "It looks like Niles will be busy for a while," he said. "I guess you can relax."

Shana yanked at a passing assistant's shirttail. "Perrier," she ordered.

He nodded. "Right away."

Shana sighed and plopped down on a gray tweed couch behind them. "That's the modeling business. Half the time, it's hurry up and then wait. At least this will be an easy shoot. There's only one change of clothes, I think. Sometimes, these shoots can be a madhouse." Shana dug into her purse and took out a mirror. She studied her face for a moment. "Perfect," she murmured. Then she took out a piece of gum and popped it into her mouth.

"A madhouse is right," Zack said with a chuckle. "You should have seen the shoot earlier in the week."

Shana looked bored. "Tough, huh?"

Zack nodded soberly. "Niles had just come back from a big job in Peru. He was doing a fashion shoot in the rain forest."

"That sounds damp," Shana said, chewing energetically. "The rain forest is *murder* on your hair."

"Anyway, when the assistants unpacked all the equipment, they found a couple of centipedes in the cases," Zack confided, leaning close to Shana.

"Ewwww," she said. "Gross. There was a spider in my kitchen the other day. I called the landlord."

"These guys were big," Zack said with a shudder. "Like this," he said, holding his thumb and third finger four inches apart. "Two hundred little squirmy legs."

"Wow," Shana said. "A centipede with two hundred legs. Amazing."

"The thing about this centipede is that it moves really fast," Zack said. "They're practically impossible to catch."

"This is getting worse and worse," Shana said. "Couldn't they use some Raid?"

"They have these superstrong genes," Zack improvised quickly. "Pesticides won't kill them. And they have this stinger in the back about this long," Zack said, indicating an inch between his thumb and forefinger.

Shana stopped chewing. "A stinger?"

Zack nodded soberly. "In Peru they call it the Stinging Diablo of Death," he confided.

"Stinging?" Shana asked in a hushed voice. "They *sting*?"

Zack nodded. "And when they do . . ." Slowly, he trailed an index finger across his throat.

"You mean . . ."

Zack nodded soberly. "Kaput."

"But that's dangerous!" Shana said, sitting up a little.

"Tell me about it," Zack agreed. He leaned closer. "It was tragic. Niles had to get new assistants."

Shana's mouth dropped open. "You mean . . ."

Zack trailed his index finger across his neck again.

"Kaput," Shana whispered.

Zack sat up. "But not to worry," he said cheerfully. "Before they . . . went, the assistants captured all the Stinging Diablos of Death."

"Well, thank goodness."

"Except one."

Shana swallowed her gum. "O-one?" she choked.

"Just one," Zack said with a shrug. "But I'm sure it's gone by now. They trapped it in the model's dressing room, but it got away. I'm positive it's already crawled away on its two hundred squirmy feet."

Shana's green eyes widened in horror. Still choking, she jerked to her feet, grabbed her makeup bag, and ran frantically out of the studio.

One of Niles's assistants walked by with a bottle of mineral water. "What happened to Shana?" he asked. "I was just bringing the drink she ordered."

Zack shook his head. "I have no idea," he said. "She just ran out."

"Ran out?" The assistant looked shocked.

Zack nodded solemnly.

"What are we going to do now?" The assistant cast a guilty look at Niles. "Niles is going to freak. We need a model."

"Hmmmm," Zack said. "Maybe I can help."

"Sorry, guy," the assistant said as he rushed off. "You just don't have the legs."

Zack whistled softly as he watched the assistant run across the studio. "But I just might know someone who does," he murmured.

Chapter 3

Zack dashed to the phone and punched out Kelly's number. He drummed a frantic rhythm on the tabletop while he counted the rings. He had already made sure that Kelly was planning to be home that morning, but there was always a chance she had decided to go for a walk or catch a few rays at the beach.

He heard the receiver being lifted. Something clunked against something. He closed his eyes in frustration. He would bet that Kelly's little brother, three-year-old Billy, had picked up the phone. *Great*, Zack thought. *Now I'll never get through.*

A baby voice piped through the receiver. "Hello?"

"Billy," Zack cooed desperately. "It's Zack. Is Kelly there?"

"I have a red truck," Billy confided.

Zack gripped the receiver. "That's great, Billy. Is Kelly there?"

"No, it's Billy. Billy, Billy, Billy."

"Billy," Zack said, trying to curb his frustration, "pul-eeze get your sister."

"I just had some apple juice, but now I want a cookie."

"Listen, kid," Zack said, "I'll buy you a carton of cookies if you put Kelly on the phone."

Suddenly Zack heard Kelly's voice in the background. He sighed in relief. "Billy, what are you doing? Is someone on the phone?"

"Kelly!" Zack shouted desperately. "Kelly, it's me! Zack!"

Kelly's warm voice came calmly through the receiver. "Zack, why are you screaming at me?"

Zack slumped against the counter. "It's Lisa," he gabbled. "She's freaked, Kelly. She really needs you."

Kelly's voice instantly changed to one of concern. "Oh, my gosh. Are you at the photography studio?"

"You've got to come right down," Zack said. "It's that big gray building on Beach Highway, across from the Taco Delight."

"But I have to be at Yogurt 4-U at twelve," Kelly protested. "It's my first day."

"What's more important, Kelly?" Zack asked sternly. "Lisa really needs you."

"Okay, okay, Zack," Kelly said. "I'm leaving right now."

Zack smiled as he hung up the phone. If everything went according to his brilliant plan, Kelly wouldn't make it to Yogurt 4-U today—or any day.

When Zack turned around, Niles Madrid was checking his cameras, frowning. The other model was already dressed in an Isidore Duncan original. She was sitting in front of the makeup mirror, leafing through a magazine while the stylist worked on her hair. Lisa was sitting in the chair next to her, looking absolutely thrilled as another stylist freshened *her* makeup.

Something bumped against Zack's leg, and he looked down to see Screech crawling on the floor. "Screech, what are you doing?" Zack hissed.

Screech looked up, his green eyes wide. "I'm looking for some pals for the Stinging Diablo," he said. "He'll probably be lonely, and I'm sure I can find him some spiders for company."

Zack reached down, grabbed Screech's shirt collar, and yanked him to his feet. "There is no Stinging Diablo of Death," he whispered fiercely.

Screech looked disappointed. "There isn't? I was going to build a special tank for him and everything."

"It's part of the plan," Zack explained.

Screech nodded in understanding. Then he frowned. "What plan?"

"Shhhh," Zack warned.

Across the studio, Niles Madrid was standing, his hands on his hips, his straight blond hair sticking up where he'd passed a furious hand through it. "What do you mean she *left*?" he demanded of the cowed assistant.

"She . . . ran out," the assistant said.

"She *ran out*?" Niles bellowed. "Shana just . . .*ran out*?"

The assistant nodded.

"And you *let* her run out?"

The assistant nodded again.

Niles rolled his eyes heavenward. "Why me?" he asked the ceiling. Then he caught sight of Isidore Duncan. "Izzy, darling, what can I say?" he said in a honeyed, frantic voice. "It's a conspiracy. They're trying to drive me crazy. We're going to have to find someone else quickly, and we *will*, I promise you. . . ."

"No sweat," Izzy said amiably. He took a swig of orange juice and winked at Lisa. She looked as though she were about to faint.

Niles wheeled around, took his assistant by the arm, and moved away from Isidore and Lisa, toward Zack. "What are we going to do?" he whispered frantically to the assistant. "I can't cancel this shoot, and we're already running over. I've got the big campaign coming up on Monday, and I haven't even made a final decision about the model. It's going to take at least an hour for the agency to send someone, and then she might be wrong. Why is this happening to me?"

"I don't know," the assistant said nervously. "I'll fix it, Niles. I'll find someone."

Niles pushed both hands through his hair. "Where are we going to find someone now?" he asked in a choked voice. "Do you think Miss Perfect is going to walk through that door and say hello?"

Just then, the door opened, and a glowing Kelly walked in. "Hello," she said.

Zack couldn't have planned it more perfectly if he'd tried. Kelly stood in the doorway, looking absolutely drop-dead gorgeous. Her long, shiny hair spilled down her back in a silky cascade. Her blue eyes were sparkling, and she flashed a shy, inviting smile. Dressed in a faded denim mini and a flowered top, she looked casual but stylish, fresh but sexy, and completely, utterly perfect. Zack had to admit he was prejudiced, but Niles Madrid seemed to find Kelly as irresistible as he did. His mouth dropped open, and he pointed.

"It's Miss Perfect," he squeaked.

"No," Kelly said nervously. "It's Miss Kapowski."

Niles turned to his assistant. "Take her to the dressing room," he babbled. "If the outfit doesn't fit, make it fit."

"It will fit," Lisa called from across the studio. "I

used Kelly as a model when I designed it."

Niles clutched his head in joy. He leaned over and kissed Kelly's hand. "Bless you," he murmured. "Now go with Roger." Then he scuttled back toward his cameras.

A bewildered Kelly looked at Zack. "What's going on?" she whispered.

"You're the model," Zack told her, giving her a push toward Roger, the assistant.

Kelly's eyes widened. "But wait, Zack. This is a big deal," Kelly said nervously. "Niles Madrid and Isidore Duncan! I can't do it. I'll freeze. Or I'll faint. Or something."

"No, you won't, Kelly," Zack said. "You can do anything you set your mind to. I believe in you." He took her by the shoulders and looked deep into her gorgeous blue eyes. "Now, knock 'em dead, kiddo."

Kelly bit her lip. "Thanks," she whispered, trying to smile.

Roger took her elbow and hustled her away toward the dressing rooms. A dazed Zack leaned back against the wall. For just a moment, Kelly had looked at him as though he were the greatest guy in the world. It had only been for a moment. But right now, even a moment was enough.

▲   ▼   ▲

"Okay, everybody. Look happy!" Niles crouched behind the camera. Lisa looked into the lens and smiled. Happy? She was absolutely ecstatic!

Niles clicked off a few shots, then popped up again. "Okay, this time, Kelly and Louann, look at the camera," he directed the two models. "And Lisa, I want you to look at Izzy. Look at him as though you adore him, darling. That's it." Niles ducked behind the camera again.

Lisa smiled into Izzy's mischievous dark eyes. She wasn't acting a bit. It had only taken her about five minutes to develop a major crush on Isidore Duncan.

She heard the whirr of the camera as Niles clicked off shots. "Okay, Lisa," he called. "You can stop looking at Izzy. Lisa? Lisa?"

"Lisa?" Izzy mimicked wickedly. His grin widened, and he winked. Niles gave up and kept on shooting while Kelly and Louann posed around Lisa and Izzy.

"I love your clothes, Lisa," Izzy said as the camera clicked furiously. "You have your own style, and that's unusual for someone so young. Your clothes just jumped out at me. You have real talent."

"Gosh," Lisa said. "Do you really think so?"

"I wouldn't say it if I didn't mean it," Izzy said. "And I wouldn't invite you to participate in my show if I didn't think so, either." He grinned. "I'm not that nice."

"I'll bet you are," Lisa protested.

He looked at her and shook his head. "You are really sweet, Lisa Turtle. I'm glad I got to meet you."

"Oh, Mr. Duncan," Lisa said with a sigh. "This has been the best day of my life."

"Call me Izzy," he said, a twinkle lighting his dark eyes. "I'm not that much older than you, you know."

"Izzy," Lisa said. She felt like swooning.

Niles stopped shooting. "That was fabulous, darlings. You can relax a minute while I reload."

"So when are you coming to San Francisco?" Izzy asked her.

"We're leaving Friday morning," Lisa explained. "I can't wait."

"You must come and see me first thing," Izzy said. "Promise? I want to show you the studio and introduce you around."

"I promise," Lisa said breathlessly. This was better than she'd ever imagined! Not only did a famous designer like her work, but he liked her, too! And Isidore Duncan was practically the cutest guy she'd ever seen in her life.

The shoot was over before they knew it. Niles shot two more rolls of film and then called a halt. "I have everything I need," he declared. Once the shoot was over, the frantic edge left his voice, and he was warm and friendly. "And it's fabulous! Thank you, everybody."

Niles walked over to Kelly. "And thanks especially to you, Kelly. You filled in like a pro."

"Thank you, Mr. Madrid," Kelly said, her eyes shining.

"Just make sure to give Roger your address before you leave," Niles continued. "Your check should arrive in a few days."

Kelly gulped. "You mean I get *paid*?"

Quickly, Zack moved in. He put a hand on Kelly's shoulder. "Heh, heh," he said. "You see how much she loves modeling, Niles? She'd do it for free!"

Niles nodded. "You can tell. I've never seen such excitement come through a lens. This girl could sell anything. Leave your pictures with Roger, too, Kelly, will you?"

"I don't have pict—," Kelly started, but Zack clapped a hand over her mouth when Niles bent down to pick up a camera. Zack dropped his hand and they both smiled when Niles straightened again.

Zack turned to Kelly. "Lucky you," he said, winking at her so that Niles couldn't see. "You have a free afternoon because that other job canceled on you."

Kelly looked puzzled. "I told them I was going to

be late, but I still have to go," she said. "The yogurt machine is wait—"

"No, they called," Zack said quickly, riding over her words. "They canceled completely." He turned to Niles. "Kelly had another big shoot this afternoon," he explained. "Big client. They rescheduled for next week," he told Kelly, winking furiously at her. Kelly only stared at him in confusion. Since she always told the truth, she had a hard time catching on to Zack's schemes.

A keen look gleamed in Niles's eyes. "You're free this afternoon?" he asked Kelly.

"She's free," Zack said quickly, before Kelly could say anything about Yogurt 4-U.

"Because I could take some test shots of you for this new campaign," Niles said thoughtfully. "If you test right, we'd shoot it on Monday. I think this could work out—as a matter of fact, I know it will. Are you interested?"

"Are you kidding?" Kelly squealed.

"We'd have to talk about the fee, of course," Zack said sternly.

"Right," Kelly said. "You'll have to talk to my agent about that." She winked back at Zack.

"This is one of my biggest clients, and it's a good-size fee," Niles said. Then he named a figure that was twice the airfare to San Francisco with plenty left over.

Kelly gulped. "That sounds—"

"—like it's in the ball park," Zack said doubtfully. "A little low, though."

Niles sighed. "Okay, okay." He named a higher fee.

Zack hesitated, but Kelly poked him hard in the back. "It's a deal," he said.

"Fantastic," Niles said. "Let me set up. I just know that Kelly is going to be perfect. Kelly, you can go find Roger and tell him you'll be testing for the new account."

As soon as Niles wandered off, Kelly threw her arms around Zack and kissed him. "You're incredible!" she said in a thrilling whisper. "That will not only pay my airfare, it's twice as much as I'd make working for the whole two weeks at Yogurt 4-U!"

"Don't mention it, Kelly," Zack said, quickly taking the opportunity to respond by slipping his arms around her. "I knew you could handle it. When that other model ran out, I called the most beautiful girl I knew to replace her."

Kelly looked at him slyly. "I wonder why that other model left so suddenly like that."

Zack shrugged innocently. "Who knows? It was just a lucky break."

"Uh-huh," Kelly said, giving him a meaningful glance. She gave him a last squeeze, then slipped out of his arms. "You're the best," she said softly. Then she ran across the studio in search of Roger.

The feel of Kelly's lips still burned against Zack's

lips and cheek. Her perfume seemed to linger around him. Zack sighed happily. His plan had worked. *Five whole days in a romantic city*, he thought. *This will be my big chance*. Zack would get her back, even if he had to stay up all night making plans. He was determined—this was going to be the best spring break ever!

Chapter 4

"Don't worry, guys," Screech assured the gang as they walked through the terminal at the Los Angeles International Airport on Friday morning. "There's only a one-in-twenty-thousand chance the plane will crash."

Luckily, everyone else was too excited to pay any attention to Screech. But Jessie rolled her eyes at Zack.

"Screech is getting out of control," she said in a low voice. "He's obsessed with this probability thing."

"I know," Zack answered. "We have to do something."

"He's driving me crazy," Jessie grumbled. "Every time I close my eyes, I see plane crashes and exploding asteroids."

Kelly had overheard them, and she hung back a bit while Slater and Lisa moved forward to show their tickets to the attendant at the gate.

"We just have to convince him that good things happen more often than bad things," Kelly said practically. "Because they really do."

Zack smiled tenderly at her. Kelly was just so sweet. "You're absolutely right, Kelly," he said.

Kelly moved forward to hand her ticket over, and Jessie arched an eyebrow at Zack. "You really have it bad," she murmured. "Don't tell me you still think you and Kelly can get back together."

Zack only smiled mysteriously. "Ask me no questions, and I'll tell you no lies," he said.

"Well, San Francisco is really romantic," Jessie said. "Who knows? She might have a temporary delusion or something." She grinned at Zack to show that she was only joking.

Who knows? Zack repeated to himself dreamily as he trooped onto the plane with the others. Unfortunately, Kelly had the seat next to Lisa, and he was stuck with Screech. But at least Kelly was directly across the aisle from him.

"I'm so excited," she told him. Then she added in an undertone, "I wouldn't be here if it weren't for you, Zack. Thanks to you, I have my college money *and* plenty left over for the trip."

"I knew you'd get the big job," Zack assured her. "Who could turn down that face?"

Kelly blushed. "I was lucky," she said.

"So what was the job, anyway?" Lisa asked, leaning over to join the conversation. "What did you have to do?"

"Model," Kelly said vaguely. "I just had to, you know, stand there and smile."

Lisa blew out an exasperated breath. "I know that. But what was the product? Clothes?"

"No," Kelly said. "Not clothes."

"Then what?" Lisa persisted.

"Just . . . a product, that's all," Kelly said.

Slater popped his head over the seat in front of Lisa and Kelly. "Was it food? Did you get any free samples?"

"Really, you guys," Kelly said. "It was nothing. It wasn't a local campaign, anyway. You won't see any of the ads in Palisades."

Zack frowned. Kelly seemed awfully evasive. "But what—," he started.

"Ooooh, we're starting to take off!" Kelly exclaimed. Her hand shot out and grabbed Zack's, her small fingers curving around his. Zack immediately forgot his question.

"Don't worry," Zack said. "We'll be perfectly safe."

"Actually—," Screech started, but Zack kicked him, and he shut up.

The engines whined, higher and higher, and the plane lifted into the air.

"We're off!" Lisa exclaimed excitedly. "I'm on the way to the greatest adventure of my life!"

The weather was perfect, and the short flight was smooth. A flight attendant passed out juice and Danish. Everyone said they were too excited to eat, but they all cleared their plates as they gazed out the window at the cerulean sky and caught an occasional glimpse of the landscape below. It seemed like no time at all before the pilot announced their approach to the San Francisco Airport.

Kelly craned out the window. "I can't see anything," she complained.

"It's too foggy," Lisa said, disappointed. "I wanted to see the Golden Gate Bridge."

The flight attendant, who was moving through the cabin, smiled at them. "We're approaching from the south, so you couldn't really see the city, anyway," she explained. "But you should have some nice views of the city as you drive in on the freeway."

"Not with this fog," Slater complained.

"We've heard that it's nice and sunny in the city," the flight attendant said. "Sometimes the airport is foggy and the city isn't at all. You know what they say about San Francisco: If you don't like the weather, walk a block."

Everyone laughed, and she moved on. "I can't wait to see Izzy," Lisa said dreamily.

"It was really nice of him to offer to pick all of us up at the airport," Kelly remarked.

"I know," Lisa said with a sigh. "He's an absolute doll."

"You'd better watch out," Kelly said with a laugh. "It looks like you're developing a pretty wicked crush."

"I think it might be too late," Lisa moaned. "It's gone beyond the development stage. I'm in a big-budget extravaganza of a crush."

The plane touched down in a perfect landing and within minutes had coasted to a stop at the gate. Down on the ground, they could see that the fog was breaking up, and patches of blue sky were visible. Everyone quickly gathered up their carry-on bags. They didn't want to miss a minute of their dream vacation!

"You see, Screech?" Zack said as they headed down the aisle. "The plane didn't crash. Here we are, safe and sound."

"There's always the ride into the city," Screech pointed out brightly.

"Screech, that's it," Lisa exploded. "I'm not going to let you spoil this vacation."

"You're going to ignore him?" Jessie asked.

"I'm going to buy him a gag," Lisa said darkly.

When they left the gate, Lisa began to look around anxiously for Izzy, but she didn't see him anywhere. "Maybe he'll meet us at the baggage claim," she guessed.

"I'm sure he'll be there," Kelly assured her, and she quickly elbowed Screech when he opened his mouth, sure that he was about to tell Lisa the percentage of chance that Izzy had forgotten.

When they got to the baggage claim, there was still no Izzy. After fifteen minutes had passed and all the other passengers had collected their luggage and moved away, they realized that their bags were missing, too.

Lisa turned to Screech. "Don't say a single word," she said. Then she sighed. "I guess we should go to the office and tell them our bags are missing. And then we need to round up a couple of taxis."

"I'm sure Izzy must be superbusy with his show," Kelly said.

"I'm sure he meant to come," Jessie said sympathetically. Lisa's soft brown eyes looked as mournful as an abandoned puppy's, and they all felt terrible for her.

Zack looked across the baggage area and saw a uniformed man patiently holding a sign. He moved closer and saw the name TURTLE.

"Hey, Lisa," Zack said. "Check that out. That guy must be for you."

"Huh?" Lisa asked. She approached the man

slowly. "I'm Lisa Turtle," she said hesitantly. "Are you here for me?"

"Yes, Miss Turtle," the man said, removing his cap. "I'm George, Mr. Duncan's driver. Can I get your bags?"

"Izzy sent a limousine?" Lisa asked incredulously.

"Yes, for you and your friends," George said. "It's right outside by the curb."

Everyone looked through the floor-to-ceiling windows. A long, black stretch limousine stood outside. Slater gave a low whistle.

"We'll be right with you, George," Lisa said composedly. He nodded, tipped his hat, and walked out toward the car.

As soon as George had passed through the electric doors, Lisa let out a squeal. "I can't believe it—a limo! That's what Izzy meant when he said he'd give me a ride to the city! I thought he was going to pick us up in his car!" Lisa sighed. "That man is just incredible."

Screech nodded in agreement. "I like George already," he said.

Now the gang didn't even mind that their baggage hadn't made it onto the right plane. They filled out the forms in record time and the clerk assured them the bags would be sent to their hotel by the afternoon. When they ran outside again,

George opened the limousine door with a flourish, and Lisa slid in first.

"I could get used to this," she remarked, sliding onto the soft leather seat.

"This is definitely my speed," Zack agreed, sliding in after her.

They all piled in, exclaiming over the rich upholstery. "There's a TV, too!" Screech said in awe.

"You see, Screech?" Kelly pointed out. "Good things happen all the time."

The smoked window rolled down between the driver's seat and the back. "There are snacks in the bar if you want them," George said. "Just press the button on the control panel."

"Thank you, George," Lisa said.

"The King Cole Hotel, miss?"

"That's right, George. And take the scenic route." Lisa smiled a queenly smile, and the smoked-glass panel slowly slid up again.

"You sound like you've been doing this all your life," Jessie said admiringly.

"Who knows?" Lisa said. "Maybe I will be."

Jessie and Kelly exchanged a concerned glance. They didn't even have to say anything—they knew exactly what the other was thinking. They'd never known Lisa to flip for a guy so completely before. Izzy was older, not to mention rich and famous. He seemed like a pretty good guy, but he could still break Lisa's heart.

There wasn't much to see outside the windows at first, but soon they began to catch glimpses of the city. George took an elevated freeway, and suddenly, they saw the whole city spread out beneath them. Most of the buildings were painted white or soft colors, and the city seemed to glow against the blue sky.

"It's gorgeous," Lisa breathed.

"What's that weird building?" Kelly asked.

"I think it's the TransAmerica pyramid," Zack said. "Isn't it cool?"

"And that big, tall building is the Bank of America," Jessie told them. She'd already been to San Francisco to visit her father. "You can go all the way up to the top. My father took me to eat there. You can't believe the view—you can see the Golden Gate Bridge *and* the Bay Bridge. And that round tower is called Coit Tower. It was built in honor of the firemen who saved the city during the big quake."

"Speaking of earthquakes, there's a one-in-seventy-five chance—," Screech started.

"Isn't this wonderful?" Kelly interrupted determinedly as George took an exit and left the freeway. "We're so lucky. And *I'm* so lucky. If I hadn't gotten that modeling job, I wouldn't be here at all."

"Speaking of that modeling job," Slater said, "you never did tell us what it was for."

Kelly bit her lip, and she looked annoyed that

she'd slipped and brought up the job at all. "I already told you, it wasn't any big deal," she said as George coasted to a stop at a red light. "Look at the way the Victorian houses are painted! They're beautiful!"

Everyone followed her pointing finger except Slater. He was squinting off into the distance, and suddenly, he burst out laughing. "I can't believe it!" he crowed.

"What are you laughing at, Slater?" Jessie asked.

Slater was laughing so hard he could barely talk. "Look!" he croaked. "It's Kelly."

Everyone craned out the window to see. "Where?" Zack asked crossly. "What are you talking about, Slater? Kelly's right here."

"Don't look down," Slater said. "Look *up*."

Everyone looked up to a billboard on a hill. Slater was right—it *was* Kelly, and she was ten feet high. She was holding a tiny hot dog in a blanket, ready to bite it, her sparkling eyes looking about as big as two wading pools.

"Oh, no!" Kelly screamed, and she hid her face in the car upholstery. "No! I can't believe it!"

Slater chuckled wickedly. "What's the matter, Kelly? Don't you like being a princess?"

Everybody's heads swiveled back to read the billboard. Right next to Kelly's big head, the bright red letters read THE PIGLET POP PRINCESS SAYS, "YUM, YUM, YUM!"

Everyone exploded into laughter. "Piglet Pop!" Lisa exclaimed, wiping at her wet eyes.

"A piglet princess in our very midst!" Jessie said, giggling.

"Should we make you a crown of little weenie hot dogs?" Slater asked.

Zack gently lifted Kelly's head from the car seat. "Kelly, what's the big deal?" he said loyally. "So you're the piglet princess. It's a legitimate product and a good campaign. Right, gang?" he asked meaningfully.

"Right," Jessie agreed quickly.

"We were just surprised at first," Lisa said. "There's no reason for you to be embarrassed."

"I don't know why you would be, anyway," Screech said. "Piglet Pops are my favorite snack."

"If you look at it a certain way, it's really an honor," Jessie said.

"Right," Slater said.

"So there's no reason to laugh," Zack said, shooting the others a warning glance. "I mean, we're proud of you, Kelly. It's not every girl who can be the princess of pig—" Zack felt a laugh bubble in his throat, but he squelched it and started again. "The princess of . . . piglets!" he finished in a howl of uncontrollable laughter. Everybody collapsed on each other and burst into gleeful howls again.

Kelly only sighed. "Okay, okay," she said ruefully. "It's just one billboard. Big deal."

Just then, George rolled to another stop at a red light. Slowly, they coasted past a huge truck. Painted on the side was Kelly, holding a Piglet Pop with that wide-eyed, dazzling smile. In big red letters, it read THE PIGLET POP PRINCESS!

"Don't say one word," Kelly warned them all sternly.

"Of course not," Jessie said.

"Your highness," Slater added. And they all burst out laughing again. But this time, Kelly joined in.

"I'm sure it's just that one billboard, Kelly," Zack said finally to reassure her. "We won't see any more."

"Absolutely," Slater said. But the two guys exchanged glances. Somehow, they had a feeling that they hadn't seen the last of the Piglet Pop princess.

Chapter 5

By the time they reached the hotel, Kelly had gotten over her embarrassment. She could never stay in a bad mood for long, and the excitement of actually being in San Francisco for the first time soon took over. Even after they'd passed three more billboards with her face on them, Kelly refused to get discouraged.

"Nobody looks at billboards, anyway, right?" she told the gang as George pulled up in front of the King Cole Hotel.

"Right," everyone chorused loyally.

"Daddy!" Jessie called as she caught sight of her father standing outside the hotel with a bouquet of spring flowers in his arms. As soon as George had stopped the car, Jessie sprang out and threw herself into her father's arms.

Everyone else scrambled out of the car and greeted Mr. Spano. Jessie looked flushed and radiant. She and her father had gone through a rocky period earlier in the year when Jessie had thought he might get back together with her mother. But he'd reconciled with his second wife, and even though Jessie hadn't been crazy about Leslie in the beginning, she had tried to warm up to her.

"It's so great of you to give us the rooms, Mr. Spano," Lisa said. "You don't know what this means to me. I think it might change my life."

"I was glad to do it, Lisa," Mr. Spano said warmly. "And I'm sorry I couldn't meet you all at the airport. The hotel has a very important guest— the queen of Lusitania."

"Wow, having royalty here is great for the hotel, Daddy," Jessie said.

"Kelly is royalty, too," Screech interjected. "She's the princess of—ow!" he exclaimed as Kelly stepped firmly on his foot.

"Just arranging the security has been a big job," Mr. Spano explained as he ushered them into the lobby. "Not to mention all the special items—down pillows and Swiss chocolates and a special bubble bath we had to fly in from Paris."

"You shouldn't have gone to all that trouble, Mr. Spano," Screech said modestly. "Regular bubble bath is fine with me."

"The hotel looks beautiful, Daddy," Jessie said, looking around. "I haven't seen it since the renovations."

The opulent lobby was decorated in red and gold, with crystal chandeliers and a deep crimson carpet. The long reception desk was marble, and velvet sofas were scattered about the oak-paneled room. Employees bustled about, looking busy and capable in their sober black uniforms. "It's like being in old San Francisco," Jessie marveled.

"That's the idea," her father said.

Zack looked at the crystal and marble and velvet and whistled. He leaned in toward Slater. "I'm sure glad the price is right," he said in a low voice.

"You said it, preppie," Slater agreed.

With Mr. Spano supervising, they were whisked through check-in in no time at all. They piled onto the elevators excitedly, eager to see their rooms.

"I arranged for a high floor," Mr. Spano explained as the elevator whooshed upward. "You'll have a fabulous view."

Mr. Spano was right. When he opened the door to the boys' room, they all gasped at the view. "Come on," Lisa said. "Let's go see ours."

Mr. Spano ushered the girls into their room next door. Immediately, Kelly, Jessie, and Lisa ran over to the windows. To the left, the deep orange of the Golden Gate Bridge was visible, the green hills of Marin beyond.

"This is so gorgeous," Kelly said. "Thank you, Mr. Spano."

"That's Sausalito on the other side of the bay," Jessie said, pointing.

"It looks beautiful," Kelly breathed. "I want to go there. My mom said it's a really cute town."

"I can't wait to go sightseeing," Jessie said, checking her watch. "We have plenty of time before dinner."

"I'm taking you all out, don't forget," Mr. Spano reminded them. "Leslie is going to meet us here at six-thirty."

"Great," Jessie said. "I can't wait to see her again." It wasn't strictly true, but Jessie was really trying to like her stepmother. And she was glad she'd said it when her father's face brightened.

"I have a very special place in mind that I think you kids will love," Mr. Spano said. "I have to run now, though." He bent over and kissed Jessie.

"See you later, Daddy," Jessie said. As soon as he left the room, she threw herself on the bed. "Isn't this the greatest?"

"Fantastic!" Kelly enthused. "Now, let's go exploring."

There was a knock on the door, and Lisa opened it. Slater, Zack, and Screech stood there, Screech with three cameras around his neck and a tour guide in his hand.

"Anybody for sightseeing?" Slater asked. "You girls had better put on your walking shoes. Mr. Spano told us that the hills are killers."

"We're ready," Kelly said, jumping up.

"You guys, I'm going to pass. I want to head over to Izzy's studio," Lisa said.

Everybody stared at Lisa. "What?" Jessie asked. "We just got here."

"I want to thank him for the limo," Lisa explained.

"Can't you just call him?" Kelly asked. "We want to go explore, Lisa."

Lisa shrugged. "So go explore. I'll catch up with you later. I really want to see Izzy."

"But, Lisa, this is spring break!" Zack protested.

"I know," she said, ushering them out. "And this is the way I want to spend it. I'll be fine. Really. You guys have fun."

Before they knew what was happening, the gang was out in the hall with a closed door between them and Lisa. They exchanged glances.

"I can't believe Lisa would turn down sightseeing," Jessie said. "She was so excited about seeing San Francisco."

"Until she met Izzy," Kelly said. "Now she's more excited about seeing *him*."

"I hope she doesn't go off the deep end," Slater observed.

"If you ask me, she's already over her head," Zack said.

▲   ▼   ▲

Lisa checked her watch. She wanted to rush right out the door and straight to Izzy's studio, but after a hectic morning of traveling, she felt pretty grungy. She ran into the marble bathroom and turned on the taps full blast. She'd take a quick bubble bath first. She'd already planned her outfit on the plane—her pleated black-and-white tweed pants with a white blouse, a blazer, suspenders, and a great tie she'd snitched from her father's closet. She'd read in a fashion magazine that Izzy had been inspired by the menswear look.

Lisa slipped on a shower cap and slipped under the fragrant bubbles. She closed her eyes. She could see it now—the husband-and-wife designer team of Isidore Duncan and Lisa Turtle. Duncan and Turtle. Or maybe just—the Duncans. Colors and fabrics swirled before Lisa's eyes as she imagined sketching with Izzy by her side. For the big fall fashion show, the press would wave notebooks in the air and crow with the triumph of the two fash-ion geniuses.

Izzy had elegance, Lisa thought dreamily. She had a sense of fun. Izzy knew how to cut on the bias. She knew how to . . . well, sew a hem. They were a perfect match!

The water had cooled, and Lisa opened her eyes and jumped out. She'd never capture Izzy's heart if she lolled in the bathtub all day!

She was dressed and ready in only fifteen minutes. Lisa pored over the map of San Francisco. Izzy's studio was on a street right near the bay. It looked like it might be walking distance, but Lisa decided to take a cab. She didn't want to arrive all sweaty.

The cab ride only took five minutes. Izzy's studio was in a converted warehouse in an industrial section of the city. But most of the buildings seemed renovated, and she could see by reading the signs that there were other designers, architects, and artists in the neighborhood. There were a few cute restaurants with outdoor cafés under bright umbrellas. The area definitely looked like a fun place to work.

Lisa pushed open the door to Izzy's building. The reception area was done in silver and gray, and Lisa recognized the receptionist's bright yellow jacket as an Isidore Duncan original. She gave her name, and the woman pushed a button on the phone.

"Lisa Turtle is here to see you," she said into the phone. A howl came through the receiver, and the receptionist smiled at Lisa. "He sounds awfully glad that you're here," she said. "You can go right on back to the workroom. Straight down the hall, turn left, then all the way to the end of the hall. You can't miss it."

"Thanks," Lisa said. She followed the directions, her heart pounding as she walked down the long hallways. Finally she came to a huge industrial door. She pushed it open and entered a room with a breathtaking close-up view of downtown San Francisco. The room was in chaos, with models running everywhere and seamstresses, their mouths full of pins and their hands full of tape measures, running after them. Bolts of fabric were unrolled on long tables, and one whole wall was full of sketches pinned up with thumbtacks.

Then Lisa saw Izzy at the end of the room. He was pinning a neckline onto a dark blue gown that one of the models was wearing, frowning in concentration. Lisa could see even from across the room how thick and luxurious the silk material was, how it draped and fell. The neckline and sleeves were made of intricate, delicate lace with a scattering of tiny crystal beads. How Lisa would love to work with material that beautiful!

Izzy stepped back and regarded the model. "That's it," he said. "Fabulous. Thank you, Arlene."

Then he turned and saw Lisa. "Lisa!" he cried, and opened his arms wide. He clapped his hands and everyone stopped talking and turned to look.

"Everybody, this is Lisa Turtle, designer of tomorrow. Lisa, this is everybody."

"Hi, everybody," Lisa said with a grin.

Izzy came forward and kissed her on the cheek. "I love your outfit," he said. "You look absolutely gorgeous."

"So do you," Lisa blurted. She couldn't help it. Izzy *did* look gorgeous, even in faded jeans and a black turtleneck. His curly hair was awry, as though he'd been running his fingers through it all day. But his deep brown eyes were twinkling as merrily as ever.

"This place is crazy," Izzy said. "Everything that could possibly go wrong today has gone wrong. I have a shipment held up at customs, and Astrid, my very best model, has taken off for Oslo to see her boyfriend. Plus the reservations for the show are completely fouled up."

"I guess it was a bad day for me to show up," Lisa said nervously.

"Don't be silly, I'm thrilled to see you. You absolutely must stay. We can—" Izzy suddenly broke off to correct a seamstress as she took in the waistline of a dress.

When Izzy came back, Lisa slipped out of her blazer. "Well, if I absolutely must stay, I'm going to pitch in and help," she said determinedly.

Izzy shook his head. "Lisa, this is your vacation," he protested. "Don't you have sightseeing to do?"

An assistant rushed in, carrying an armload of papers. "Here are the reservation letters," she said. "You wanted to see them."

"No," Izzy said. "I wanted you to *find* them, and I wanted *you* to read them and check them against the confirmation list."

"But I have your morning mail here for us to go over. You might want to read it yourself today. There's some personal stuff—"

"Katrina," Izzy snapped, "I don't have time for this today!"

"Excuse me," Lisa put in. Izzy didn't seem like the sort of person who would get angry easily. His eyebrows came down, and he looked almost scary. "I can help. That is, if it's okay."

"Is this the new apprentice?" Katrina asked.

"No," Izzy said with a sigh. "The new apprentice quit this morning. Her boyfriend asked her to fly to Europe with him. Maybe she'll bump into Astrid."

"I can help, though," Lisa told Katrina. "What do you need?"

"Great." Katrina gave a brief, harassed smile. "All you have to do is check the confirmations against the invitation list. Then type out the names of who *isn't* coming and show it to Izzy. He can make some last-minute phone calls to anybody important."

"I'd be happy to," Lisa said.

"And if you wouldn't mind, you can read the mail to me while I'm working on the models," Izzy said. "That would save me some precious time."

"No problem," Lisa said happily.

"Hold on a minute," Izzy said. "Are you sure?"

Lisa looked into the warmest brown eyes she'd ever seen. "I'm sure."

"Then you are an angel. Katrina, make sure Lisa gets a soda, or tea, or whatever. After you finish the reservation list, come to me, and we'll do the mail. I have to run." Izzy started away after flashing a smile at Lisa, but he came back a few seconds later. "And to thank you, I'd love to take you to dinner tonight," he said.

Lisa gulped as she thought of Jessie, Kelly, Zack, Slater, and Screech. She knew that they were all looking forward to Mr. Spano's special dinner, and she had been, too. But at that moment, she couldn't imagine why. Her friends seemed very far away, and this was exactly where she wanted to be. "I'd love it," she said. "It's a date."

Chapter 6

"It's the princess of Piglet Pop!" someone squealed.

Kelly hid her face in Zack's shoulder. "Not again," she groaned.

"Gee, Kelly," Slater said, taking a bite of his crab cocktail. "You're a real celebrity. This is exciting."

"It's awful," Kelly moaned.

They were all sitting in a small outdoor café on Fisherman's Wharf. Lured by the crab cocktails and crab salads, they had paused to order a snack in the courtyard of the Cannery, one of several renovated factory buildings along the wharf full of great little shops and restaurants. The crabs were sweet and delicious, the sourdough bread incredibly fresh, and the sights around them were amazing. Everything would have been perfect if only they weren't interrupted every five minutes by someone asking Kelly if she was *really* the Piglet Pop princess.

Zack noticed two young guys sitting a few tables away staring at Kelly. They could be staring at her because she was beautiful, but they could also be ready to ask her if she could get them some free Piglet Pops. He decided it was time to go.

He stood up. "If you've finished stuffing your face, Slater, we have plenty of other things to see."

Slater spooned up the last bite of his crab cocktail and tore off a piece of sourdough bread. "Hey, a growing boy like me needs nourishment," he said. "But, as a matter of fact, I am done."

Jessie poked affectionately at his stomach. "If you're not careful, you'll be growing, all right," she teased. "You had a bag of chocolate-chip cookies and a soft pretzel before that crab cocktail."

Slater flexed a muscle and flashed his dimples at Jessie. "It keeps me strong for you, momma," he said.

Screech stood up. "I can't eat anything, anyway. I miss Lisa too much. I wish she wasn't so dedicated to her fashion career. She should make time for love."

The rest of them exchanged glances, but no one was about to clue Screech in on what lay behind Lisa's sudden career-mindedness.

Kelly stood up next to Zack. "So where to next, guys?"

"How about a sundae at Ghirardelli Square?" Slater suggested. "It's just a couple of blocks from here."

Jessie groaned. "I thought you said you were done."

"Hey, I didn't have dessert yet," he said.

"A sundae sounds great to me," Screech agreed.

"I'm kind of full," Kelly said hesitantly. "And if we have sundaes, we won't be able to get to Sausalito and back on time."

"We can go to Sausalito another day," Jessie suggested.

Kelly nodded, but she looked disappointed. Zack was seized with an inspiration.

"I couldn't eat any ice cream, either," he said. "Why don't you guys go to Ghirardelli Square, and Kelly and I can take the ferry to Sausalito. We'll meet back at the hotel."

"We should stick together," Slater started, but Jessie poked him. "But I don't see why we can't split up for a few hours," he amended quickly.

"Great!" Zack said. "I mean, is it okay with you, Kelly?"

"Sure," Kelly said. "I really wanted to see Sausalito today."

Just then, an older guy ambled by, carrying a shopping bag full of groceries. "Oh, my gosh," he said, pointing at Kelly. "It's . . . it's . . . the Piglet Pop girl!" He bent over and began to rummage in the bag. "Can I have your autograph?" he asked, holding out a box of frozen Piglet Pops.

Kelly turned bright red. "I don't think I have a pen," she said quietly. The man had attracted attention, and people were really starting to notice Kelly. She wanted to sink through the floor.

Screech dug into his pocket and handed her one. "Here you go, Kelly."

Blushing all the while, Kelly quickly scrawled her name on the frozen package. "Get me out of here," she said in an undertone to Zack.

"Right away," he murmured. "Okay," he said, "we really had better be going."

"Right," Jessie said. "We'll meet you back at the hotel."

Zack took Kelly's hand, and they quickly threaded their way through the tables to the street.

"Be sure to wear a life preserver!" Screech called after them.

▲   ▼   ▲

Once they were safely on the ferry, with the breeze blowing through Kelly's silky hair, Zack turned to her.

"This is nice," he said.

Kelly nodded. "It's beautiful."

He hadn't been talking about the scenery, but he

let it pass. He looked back over the sparkling bay
toward the green hills. Then he turned around and
regarded the white city retreating behind them as
the ferry chugged across the bay.

"I wouldn't mind living here someday," he remarked. "It's such a cool city."

"I'd like it," Kelly agreed. "I think it's definitely
prettier than L.A."

"And the air is certainly cleaner," Zack said,
taking a big whiff.

Kelly laughed. "That's for sure."

The ride was short, and in less than a half hour,
they were docking in Sausalito. As they walked out
on the dock, Zack looked back at the ferry and
noticed the same two young guys who had been
checking out Kelly in the Cannery café. But now
they didn't seem to be looking at her at all, so he
relaxed. He'd finally gotten Kelly away from the
competition at Bayside High, and he wasn't about
to lose her to a long-distance romance!

For the next hour, Zack and Kelly wandered the
streets of Sausalito, poking into quaint shops and
galleries and admiring the Victorian houses. Kelly
bought souvenirs and Zack picked out some post-
cards. It was an easy, relaxed afternoon, and Zack
couldn't help wishing that it would be this easy to
recapture Kelly. He was longing to say something,
anything, that would get Kelly to commit to their
relationship again. But he didn't want to push her.

He'd made that mistake before, and once was more than enough.

There was still time before the return ferry, so Kelly and Zack headed down Bridgeway, the main street, past the shops and restaurants and along the marinas that hugged the shore. The pleasant sounds of lines clanking against their masts wafted in the soft air as they wandered down the street.

"What a neat town," Kelly said. "It must be so much fun to live here and take the ferry to work in the city."

"Except in a storm," Zack said.

Kelly laughed. "Now you sound like Screech," she teased.

Their footsteps slowed when they came to an odd-looking marina. Here, there were houseboats instead of sailboats. But these were like no houseboats Zack had ever seen. They were more like strangely constructed floating houses. They were fun and fantastic, and Kelly giggled in delight when she saw them.

"Isn't this great?" she asked. "It looks like people actually live in these. Let's go explore them."

They wandered down the dock, laughing at the different houseboats and pointing out favorite ones.

"Wouldn't it be fun to live on one?" Kelly asked, her eyes shining.

"I don't know," Zack said, giving an eccentric wooden structure a dubious look. "I think I'd be seasick all the time. They look pretty shaky."

"I think it would be cozy," Kelly said. "And romantic, too. Can you imagine how snug you'd feel with the fog rubbing against the windows and the foghorn hooting?"

Zack started to say that just about anyplace would be romantic with Kelly around, but he stopped. He couldn't believe it—the same guys that had been at the café and on the ferry were sitting on a houseboat a couple of yards away. Now they *were* looking at Kelly again, and one of them nudged the other one.

Kelly began to wander farther toward them, and Zack hurried after her. All she needed was to be asked for another autograph. That would definitely spoil the romantic mood!

But he was too late. "Hey," the guy with the dark hair said. "Aren't you the Piglet Pop model?"

Kelly must have been getting used to it by now, because she smiled and didn't blush. "Yes," she admitted.

"I thought so," he answered, and the other one nodded.

"You don't have a frozen package of piglets for me to autograph, do you?" Kelly asked in a teasing tone.

"No," the dark-haired guy said shortly. He frowned. "I don't."

They sure weren't as friendly as Kelly's fans usually were. Maybe they were nervous around her.

"Come on, Kelly," Zack urged. "It's time to catch the ferry."

With a last smile, Kelly turned and followed Zack back to the road. "I'm looking forward to dinner tonight, aren't you?" she asked as they headed toward the ferry landing.

"You bet," Zack said. He wasn't being strictly truthful, though. He'd much rather stay and have dinner alone with Kelly in one of the romantic floating restaurants right on the Sausalito waterfront. But at this rate, even at a tiny corner table lit by candlelight, someone would probably barge in and ask Kelly if she was the Piglet Pop princess. *Being Prince Charming to a princess isn't easy,* Zack thought as he made his way onto the ferry. *Not by a long shot.*

▲   ▼   ▲

That night, Mr. Spano took the gang out to a fabulous restaurant in a converted diner. It gleamed with mahogany and brass and romantic lighting. There was plenty of laughter as they ate the delicious food and passed their desserts around so that everyone could have a taste of each. Even Jessie and Leslie, her stepmother, got along.

Everyone was still flushed and laughing as they

entered the lobby of the hotel. Everyone except Screech. Ever since they'd come back from sight-seeing and gotten the message that Lisa would be eating dinner with Isidore Duncan, he'd been sunk in gloom.

He stopped as the gang headed for the elevators. "I'm going to hang out down here for a while," he told them.

Zack gave him a sympathetic look. "Going to wait up for Lisa?" he asked.

"Not at all," Screech protested huffily. "I just want some hot chocolate."

Kelly's blue eyes were full of sympathy as she patted his shoulder. "Okay, Screech. See you to-morrow morning."

Everyone said good-night, and Screech headed off toward the coffee shop. *They're all wrong,* he thought irritably. He wasn't waiting up for Lisa. He really *did* want a hot chocolate. But he made sure to choose a seat in the coffee shop that faced the glass door into the lobby. If Lisa walked in, he could ride up in the elevator with her.

Screech stirred his hot chocolate miserably, wait-ing for the marshmallows to melt. He couldn't seem to shake this sense of doom and gloom. He had been proven right. The plane hadn't crashed, but they'd lost their luggage. Of course, it had been delivered that afternoon, but then Lisa had gone off with Isidore Duncan and hadn't been seen since.

No matter what little good thing happened, some big bad thing always came along and squashed the little thing flat.

Screech sighed as he scooped up a gooey marshmallow. He used to have a happy feeling in his heart almost all the time. But not anymore. Ever since his math teacher, Mr. Sandusky, had introduced him to the science of probability, he'd spent all his time calculating the odds for disaster. It was a depressing way to spend your time, but he couldn't seem to help it. The world had suddenly turned into a very treacherous place.

Screech finished his hot chocolate and ordered another one. He leaned back against the booth with another heavy sigh. He wished he could see Lisa's pretty face. Maybe that would cheer him up.

Then he heard a low voice come from the booth behind him. "You can't chicken out on me now, Pete," the voice said. "We've got to do it."

"I know, I know," another voice said. "But we could get in big trouble. What if we get caught?"

"We won't get caught," the low voice continued. "We've planned everything perfectly, haven't we?"

The hairs on the back of Screech's neck rose. It sounded like these guys were planning some sort of crime! *Too bad I left my Sherlock Holmes hat back in Palisades*, he thought. Screech pressed back against the booth, straining to hear more.

"I just don't know," the second guy fretted.

"Don't be such a weasel," the first guy said. "You know we're doing it for our cause. Her Highness deserves everything she gets."

Screech's hand flew to his mouth to stop the gasp that threatened to emerge. They were going to do something to the queen of Lusitania!

"You're right," the second guy said. "Okay, I'm still in."

"Okay, good," the first guy said, relieved. "Tomorrow, we kidnap the royal one. You remember the plan?"

"Sure."

Every muscle in Screech's body tensed. He held his breath. He just had to hear the plan! He waited for them to say more, but there was only silence. Maybe they were drawing something on the placemat. After they left, he could leap up and grab it and take it to the police. Screech waited and waited. Were they talking in sign language?

Finally, Screech pushed his napkin off the table and leaned over to pick it up. He gave a quick glance behind him. The booth was empty! Then he saw that there was another exit to the coffee shop— it led to the street outside.

Screech ran to the door, but the sidewalk was crowded with people, and it was impossible to tell who had been speaking. Was it the evil-looking middle-aged man on the corner? The guy with the cap over his eyes, carrying a newspaper? The dapper-looking businessman unfolding a map?

Screech moaned aloud in frustration. Suddenly, everybody looked suspicious, but there was no way to tell who was bad. All he knew was that tomorrow, someone was going to kidnap the queen of Lusitania, and it was up to him to foil the plan!

Chapter 7

Lisa yawned as she took the last order form from the typewriter. It was almost nine o'clock, and she'd been at Izzy's studio since noon. She hadn't minded a bit, though. Most of the time she'd been following Izzy around, reading to him from his correspondence or taking notes on memos he wanted her to type up for him. She had gotten a good look at Izzy at work, and she was thrilled by the whole experience.

She'd always loved the Isidore Duncan line, even though she could never afford it. Now that she saw the hard work, inspiration, and pure genius that went into it, she was more impressed than ever. Izzy was everywhere, cajoling, demanding, joking, fixing a pleat here and a neckline there until every single detail was perfect. He was absolutely the most fantastic person she'd ever met. But it wasn't just getting to see Izzy in action that had made the day so special. It was getting a firsthand look at how the fashion business worked.

A brown paper bag landed on the desk in front of her, and Lisa looked up to see Izzy grinning down. "When I promised you dinner, I was thinking of a restaurant. But it's late, and I have to be here for a while. Would you mind some take-out?"

"I won't turn it down," Lisa admitted with a grin. "I'm starving."

Izzy began pulling out containers from the bag. "There's a great little place down the street that delivers. I have lobster salad, chicken tarragon, onion rolls, and some vegetable thing so we don't feel guilty. Oh, and salad. And chocolate raspberry torte for dessert."

"It sounds heavenly," Lisa said, opening a soda. Izzy handed her a fork and a napkin and began to dish out the food.

"I'm really sorry about today," he said, looking down at the food. "Not to mention tonight. Did you have plans with your friends?"

"No," Lisa lied brightly. She'd called and left a message at the hotel that she couldn't make dinner, and she knew she'd catch some flak from everyone when she returned.

"Well, you were a big help today," Izzy said, handing her a plate. "I couldn't have done it without you. You really have a flair for design, Lisa."

"Thanks," Lisa said, blushing a little.

"Do you want to do it professionally, or is designing just a hobby?" Izzy asked curiously.

"Well, I wasn't sure before," Lisa admitted, forking up a bite of salad. "Actually, my parents want me to go to medical school. They're both doctors. But I'm a lot more interested in art and design than I am in science. They've never really understood my interest in fashion, so I guess I thought it wasn't really a good career plan, either. This is the first time I've wondered if they're wrong."

"It's hard to buck your parents, that's for sure," Izzy said. "My old man was an electrician, and when I turned eighteen, he took me down to the union hall. You can't imagine how embarrassed he was about my becoming a fashion designer."

"What about now?" Lisa asked, taking a bite of chicken.

Izzy shrugged. "He died a couple of years ago, before I made it big. He never accepted my being a designer. When he was alive, I used to think that he'd be proud of me if I was a success. But now I don't think it would have made a difference. He just couldn't accept it. I mean, the cover of *Vogue* isn't exactly *Sports Illustrated*."

Lisa's heart went out to Izzy. Suddenly, he looked so vulnerable. "What about your mom?" she asked softly.

Izzy brightened immediately. "She's great. She's totally supportive. I bought her a condo on Telegraph Hill, and she picks a different outfit of mine every day to wear on her walk down to the grocery store. She's a sixty-year-old dynamo."

"So that's where you get your energy," Lisa said with a laugh.

"I guess so," Izzy admitted. He cocked his head and looked at her. "You know what? You're really easy to talk to," he said softly.

Lisa's breath caught in her throat. There was an admiring look in Izzy's eyes that made her heart pound. She wished that he would fall for her the way she had for him. The moment lingered, and she paused, her fork in the air, waiting, held spellbound by Izzy's dark gaze.

Izzy cleared his throat. "Eat your vegetables," he ordered.

Lisa sighed and speared a green bean with her fork. *Does he think of me as a child?* she wondered.

"You know," Izzy continued, taking a thoughtful sip of mineral water, "you really have a knack for this business, Lisa. Not only are you a good designer, you hold up well under pressure. You can take notes, read my mail to me, and tell me I chose the wrong shoes for an outfit at the same time."

Lisa blushed. "I didn't mean to butt in," she said.

Izzy grinned. "I asked what you thought, and

you told me. You weren't afraid. You don't know how valuable that makes you." Izzy paused and studied her for a moment. "That's why I want to offer you a job," he said.

Lisa's fork hung in midair. "You *what*?"

"I'm offering you a job as an apprentice," Izzy said. "You'd have to start at the bottom, but I guarantee you have a future. Soon I'll be starting to work on my resort collection, and I think you could be very helpful."

"You mean you want me to start now?"

"Well, as soon as you can move up here," Izzy said, taking a bite of lobster salad.

Lisa stared at him. "But, Izzy, I'm not eighteen yet. I'm still in high school. And I'm supposed to go to college next year."

Izzy waved his fork in indifference. "Don't worry. I could find you a place to live with some of the other girls. They're models, and they live with the head of the agency. It's very respectable. When do you turn eighteen?"

"In July," Lisa said.

"You see? That's not very far away."

Lisa swallowed. "But what about school?" she asked in a low voice.

"I never graduated from high school, let alone college," Izzy said with a shrug. He put down his fork and leaned over the table toward her. "Look, Lisa. If you want to be a doctor or a lawyer or a teacher, school makes sense. But if you want to be a designer, it's just a waste of time. You get better by *doing*. Experience is the best teacher when it comes to design. I started as an apprentice when I was your age, and by twenty-one, I had my own business. Now I'm twenty-six and I'm famous. Do you think I would have been able to build my own company if I'd been in school?"

"No," Lisa admitted. "But, Izzy, my life always had a plan. And dropping out of high school isn't part of that plan. I can't imagine doing it."

"You could get your equivalency degree," Izzy said. "You could probably pass the test right now if you had to."

"But I have to go to college," Lisa said. "My parents would freak if I didn't. It's scary, Izzy."

"I know," he said. "It *is* scary. But you need courage to be fabulous, sweetheart. No guts, no glory, right?" He put his hand on top of hers. "Look, nobody can tell you what to do. I know it's a huge decision, and I don't want to pressure you. My offer is on the table. Will you at least think about it?"

Lisa nodded. "I'll think about it," she said slowly.

▲   ▼   ▲

Lisa slipped into the hotel room at eleven o'-clock. Dressed in their pajamas, Kelly and Jessie were flipping through the cable channels looking for something to watch.

"Hi," Lisa said cheerfully.

"Did you have a nice dinner?" Jessie asked. Her voice didn't sound too friendly. Lisa knew it hadn't been the nicest thing in the world to cancel out on Mr. Spano's big dinner.

"Izzy brought in some take-out," she told them while she hung up her jacket. "How was the restaurant?"

"It was fantastic," Kelly said. "I've never had such delicious food in my life. And afterward, we walked through North Beach, this wonderful section with lots of coffeehouses. We had cappuccino outside in a café. It was so much fun."

"It sounds great," Lisa said. "I wish I could have come."

"How was your day?" Jessie asked grudgingly.

Lisa sat cross-legged on the bed. "It was fantastic. I got to help Izzy. I wrote about a million memos, and helped him with his mail, and did all sorts of other things. Izzy says I really have a flair for the business. Actually, he—"

But she didn't get a chance to finish. "You mean you *worked* all day?" Jessie blurted.

Lisa nodded. "I wanted to," she said in a small

voice. "It was fun. I think I've finally found what I want to do with my life."

"But this is your vacation, Lisa," Kelly said. "It's not really fair of Izzy to draft you like that."

"Why not?" Lisa said irritably. "I was glad to do him a favor."

"A favor? It sounds like slave labor to me," Jessie said, tossing her curly ponytail behind her shoulder.

"Lisa," Kelly said more gently, "are you sure you're thinking this through? You really seem to be falling for this guy. He's older than you, and he's famous."

Lisa sprang to her feet. "You guys aren't listening to me. It's not just Izzy. And just what are you saying, that a guy as great as Izzy couldn't possibly be interested in me?"

"That's not what I mean," Kelly protested.

"Well, for your information, Izzy offered me a job," Lisa said. *Darn!* she thought. *I didn't mean to blurt it out that way.*

"What do you mean?" Jessie asked, frowning. "How can you work for Izzy? It's not exactly commuting distance."

"I wouldn't commute," Lisa explained. "I'd live here. Izzy can get me a room in a house with some models. I'd start out as an apprentice. It's an incredible opportunity," she said defensively. Kelly and Jessie were gazing at her as if she had horns growing out of her head.

"Wait a second," Jessie said. "Are we talking about leaving school?"

"If I want to be a designer, it's the only way," Lisa said.

"It's not the only way," Kelly said. "I can't believe I'm hearing this. You'd forget about college, too?"

Lisa nodded. "Izzy didn't go to college," she said. "None of the top designers did. They all started out as apprentices, working with famous designers. And now Izzy is offering me that chance."

"You mean you might say *yes*?" Jessie demanded incredulously.

Lisa sprang to her feet. "Yes, I might," she said angrily. "And obviously, you guys think it's a stupid idea."

"He's telling you to drop out of high school," Jessie said bluntly. "I call that stupid."

"Lisa, it's a big decision," Kelly said more gently. "We're just concerned, that's all. And are you sure you aren't thinking about this because you have a crush on the guy?"

Lisa felt like crying. They just didn't understand. Couldn't they see that this was the opportunity of a lifetime? "I'm going to wash up," Lisa murmured.

"We can talk more tomorrow," Jessie said stiffly.

"We're meeting the guys for breakfast at nine, and then we thought we'd take the boat to Alcatraz for the tour."

Lisa bit her lip. "I can't. Tomorrow afternoon is the fashion show."

"We'll be back before lunch," Kelly said. "I have to get ready, too. I'm modeling, remember?"

"But I'm taking notes for Izzy at a breakfast meeting tomorrow," Lisa said. "I'll just meet up with you guys at the show."

"Sure," Jessie said shortly. "Maybe we'll see you there." Lisa could tell she was still angry.

With a sigh, Lisa turned toward the bathroom. She closed the door behind her and turned on the taps full blast. Taking a washcloth, she began to scrub her face vigorously. Maybe if she rubbed hard enough, she wouldn't cry. This was the first time ever she hadn't been able to talk to Kelly and Jessie. She'd have to pour out her feelings onto the pages of her journal instead. This had been the best day and the worst day of her life. She'd finally found what she wanted to do with her life, but she'd lost her friends in the process.

Chapter 8

Screech waited until the next morning in the coffee shop to tell the rest of the gang, minus Lisa, what he had overheard the night before. Zack and Slater had already been asleep when he got back to the room the night before. Since there was nothing they could have done that night, he'd just gone to bed, too.

Zack whistled. "Wow. This is incredible. You've overheard a plot to kidnap the queen of Lusitania!"

"Are you sure you heard right, Screech?" Slater asked, a dubious note creeping into his voice. "Maybe you imagined it."

"Of course I heard right," Screech answered, insulted. "Don't you think I know the difference between fantasy and reality?"

Zack, Slater, Kelly, and Jessie exchanged

glances. "Do you really want us to answer that?" Zack asked.

"Screech, you have to be absolutely positive," Kelly said. "This is superimportant."

"Of course I'm positive," Screech said. "The two guys said they were going to kidnap the queen today!"

"We have to do something," Jessie declared. "The royal visit is a big deal for my dad. It would look terrible if the queen got kidnapped. He could even lose his job!"

"Screech, you have to tell Mr. Spano *exactly* what you heard," Zack decided. "We'll go with you."

"Well, I'm not leaving this hotel today," Jessie said. "And maybe you should stay, too, Screech. You could spot two men that look familiar."

"Zack and I will stay, too," Kelly said.

Jessie looked relieved. "You will?"

Kelly nodded. "We wouldn't have any fun sight-seeing, anyway."

"We'll all stay," Slater said, putting a comforting arm around Jessie's shoulder. "It's all for one and one for all."

"Except for Lisa," Jessie said grimly.

"Come on, Jess," Kelly said gently. "Lisa doesn't know about the kidnapping plot. She left before Screech came down to breakfast."

"She should still be here," Jessie insisted stonily.

Zack frowned. Obviously, something major was going down between the girls. But there really wasn't time to discuss it now. "Come on, gang," he said, standing up. "Let's find Mr. Spano. And then let's put our heads together and figure out the details of Operation Stakeout. Maybe we can be the ones to catch the kidnappers red-handed!"

▲   ▼   ▲

"I'm so glad you could help me out this morning," Izzy told Lisa after the breakfast meeting. "It's going to be a hectic day, but the first meeting went pretty smoothly, at least."

"I'm sure you'll have a smash hit this afternoon," Lisa told him as she closed her notebook. The meeting had been in the conference room at Izzy's studio. It was a long room with windows overlooking the huge Bay Bridge and the sparkling water of the bay. The hills of Berkeley and Oakland were visible across the expanse of blue water.

Izzy crossed his fingers, then his eyes. Lisa giggled.

"You were a big help in the meeting," he said. "I can't believe you remembered how I accessorized all those outfits."

"It was easy," Lisa said with a laugh. "I always remember clothes."

"So have you thought any more about my offer?"
Izzy asked.

Lisa looked down at the notes she'd taken that
morning. She looked down the length of the maple
conference table, then out at the beautiful blue
bay. She'd gotten over her misery of last night.
Whenever she was in Izzy's studio, she felt busy,
and needed, and *right*. She belonged here. She belonged in this business. She'd never felt so strongly
about anything in her life.

But she was scared. Her heart was beating so
fast, she could barely breathe. Did she really have
it—the courage that Izzy was talking about? The
courage to be fabulous?

"Yes," she said slowly. "I thought about it a lot."

"And?" Izzy prompted.

Lisa took a deep breath. "And I accept."

▲   ▼   ▲

Mr. Spano was shocked when he heard Screech's
story, and he immediately called the head of security and had Screech repeat it. The two men decided to beef up security and ask the queen to
remain in her suite for the day. Then they thanked
Screech and ushered the gang outside.

"Thank you," Mr. Spano told them. "We'll take
care of it from here. I'll see you later," he told

Jessie. Then the heavy oak door to his office closed, and they were left in the hall.

"Okay," Zack said. "Now it's our turn. Screech, you stay in the lobby and check out everyone who comes in. Slater and I will stake out the queen's floor. Jessie and Kelly, you help Screech in the lobby. There will be a lot of people coming and going."

They all separated to go to their posts. It was a frustrating morning, however. Zack and Slater were caught by security. The two beefy men refused to listen to their explanation and hauled them off to Mr. Spano's office, where Jessie's dad merely sighed and told them to go sightseeing and leave the security arrangements to him. In the lobby's most comfortable chair, Screech nodded off twice, and Kelly and Jessie had to keep watch and make sure he didn't fall asleep again.

"I didn't sleep a wink last night," Screech offered by way of explanation. "I was awake all night, worrying."

"I'm getting tired, too," Kelly admitted. "These couches are too comfortable."

"We have to stay alert," Jessie said. "Maybe some food will help."

"I'm going to get a breath of fresh air," Kelly said. "I'll be right back."

Kelly exited through the revolving door, and

Zack and Slater wandered over to the couches. "See anything?" Slater asked.

Jessie sighed. "Nothing."

She looked so woebegone that Slater leaned over and kissed her cheek. "Don't worry," he reassured her. "Your father has everything under control."

"That's for sure," Zack said, rubbing his elbow where one of the security agents had grabbed him.

Just then, Lisa entered the lobby and caught sight of them. She hurried over. "Hi," she said cheerfully. "I thought I'd come back and see if I could talk you guys into an early lunch. I have something to tell you. Then I have to get back to the studio. The show is at four, and it's a madhouse over there."

"Nice of you to make time for us," Jessie sniffed.

Lisa looked hurt. "This *is* a big day for me, Jessie," she said.

"Jessie didn't mean it," Slater said, giving Jessie a meaningful glance. "She's worried about her dad."

Instantly, Lisa's dark eyes were full of concern. "Why? What happened?"

Quickly, Zack filled her in on the kidnapping plot. Lisa shook her head. "This is totally amazing," she said. "I hope they catch the two men."

"Well, there's no reason we can't break for lunch," Zack said philosophically. "We can eat in the lobby restaurant and still keep an eye out."

"Sounds like a good idea," Jessie admitted. "I *am* kind of hungry."

"Where's Kelly?" Lisa asked. "I have to give her instructions about this afternoon. She's supposed to come early so I can accessorize her outfit. Everything has to be perfect."

"She went outside for some air," Screech said. "She probably went across the street to the square."

"I'll get her," Zack offered. "I'll meet you guys in the restaurant."

Zack hurried outside and crossed the street to Union Square. The early lunch crowd was beginning to form. There were office workers with brown-bag lunches and tired shoppers with overstuffed shopping bags. A musician played a violin in one corner of the square. But there was no sign of Kelly.

Zack circled the square, but he still didn't see her. She wasn't window-shopping on any of the streets lining the square, either. Maybe he had just missed her going back to the hotel. He knew that with Operation Stakeout in place, Kelly wouldn't go far.

Zack searched the lobby, but Kelly wasn't there, either. Finally, he pushed open the door to the lobby restaurant the gang had picked, called the

Sandwich Board. They had already staked out a table, but two chairs were empty. Zack hurried over.

"I can't find Kelly," he said, frowning. "She's not in the square."

"That's weird," Jessie said. "She said she'd be right back, and that was about fifteen minutes ago."

"Maybe she went back to the room," Screech guessed.

"I'll check," Zack said.

Jessie stood. "I'll come with you."

Frowning, Slater stood up, too. "I'll come, too," he said. "This is kind of weird. It isn't like Kelly to disappear."

Lisa and Screech stood up as well, and the whole gang headed for the elevators. They didn't say a word as they watched the indicator light flash the different floors.

"This is so silly," Lisa said nervously. "I'm sure she's just fine. She probably went to get a sweater or something."

"Of course," Jessie chimed in. But they couldn't disguise the uneasiness in their voices.

They hurried down the hall to the girls' room. Zack knocked on the door.

"Kelly?" he shouted. "It's us. Are you in there?"

He exchanged a worried glance with Jessie.

Then Jessie took out her card key and unlocked the door. They all walked in. The room was empty, and so was the bathroom.

Slater broke the silence. "Lisa's right. This is ridiculous. We're all worrying about nothing." He tried to laugh. "I'm sure Kelly is downstairs in the lobby right now, looking for us."

Jessie turned. "Slater's right," she said. "We should just—"

Jessie broke off with a sudden cry. A piece of paper had been thrust under the door, but they had charged into the room so fast that nobody had noticed it. "A note," she said with relief. "Now we'll find out where she is."

Jessie picked up the paper and scanned it quickly. Slowly, her face drained of color. When she looked up, the gang could see the horror in her eyes.

"Jessie, what is it?" Zack asked urgently, a terrible feeling clutching his stomach.

Jessie held out the note with a shaking hand. "Kelly's been kidnapped!" she exclaimed.

Chapter 9

Zack quickly read the note and numbly handed it to Slater. "It's true," he said.

Zack's brain seemed to be frozen. For a moment, he couldn't even think. The words on the note were burned into his memory, filling him with icy fear.

Don't bother looking for your princess. She's safe with us—for now. She'll stay safe if you keep your mouth shut and wait for instructions.

"This is nuts," Slater said after he'd read the note. "Why would anyone want to kidnap Kelly?"

"It looks like they're going to hold her for ransom," Lisa said, reading the note over Slater's shoulder.

"But why?" Jessie asked. "Kelly's parents don't have any money. And we certainly don't."

"Maybe they *think* she has money," Screech pointed out.

"Oh, my gosh!" Jessie exclaimed. "Maybe they think she's the queen!"

"But that doesn't make any sense," Zack objected. "The queen's picture has been in all the papers. They'd have to be incredibly stupid to mistake Kelly for a fifty-year-old."

"Plus the queen has blond hair," Screech offered. "Kelly's a brunette."

"Maybe they recognized her from the billboards," Slater guessed. "They might have thought she was a glitzy model."

"It's so weird that there were two kidnapping plots in one hotel," Screech said.

"Or maybe they couldn't get at the queen, so they went after Kelly," Lisa said.

"Wait a second," Zack said suddenly. He whirled on Screech. "Screech, think hard. What *exactly* did those two guys in the coffee shop say?"

"That they were going to kidnap the queen," Screech said patiently. "I told you."

"Did they *say* the queen?" Zack persisted. "Tell me what they said, word for word."

Screech frowned. "Hmmmm. Okay. They said, 'Her Highness deserves everything she gets.' And, 'Tomorrow, we kidnap the royal one.' You see? The queen."

Zack snapped his fingers. "Not the queen," he

said. "The *princess*. They were after Kelly all along!"

"But we're back where we started from," Jessie said. "Why? Why would anyone kidnap the princess of little hot dog hors d'oeuvres?"

"I don't know," Zack said. "But I have a feeling we're going to find out. Jessie, will you stay here and wait in case they call? I'd like to do a little investigating downstairs."

"Maybe we should tell my dad," Jessie said worriedly.

"Not yet," Zack said. "We can't endanger Kelly, Jessie. What if the kidnappers have people watching his office?"

"But, Zack, we can't do this alone," Lisa said. "I'd die if anything happened to Kelly."

Zack took her by the shoulders. "Don't you think I feel the same way, Lisa?" he asked, intensity burning in his hazel eyes.

Lisa gulped. "I know you do," she said softly.

"That's why we have to just chill out for a few hours until we hear from them," Zack explained. "After that, if we can't handle it, we'll go to Jessie's dad. Is everyone agreed?" He looked from face to face. Everyone looked worried and scared, but they nodded.

"Good. Screech, Lisa, Slater, let's go. Jessie, we'll be back as soon as we can. Keep a pad and pencil by the phone, and if they call, take as many notes as you can. You have to remember every detail."

"But shouldn't you wait until they call?" Jessie asked, wringing her hands.

"If we wait, the lunch crowd on Union Square will be gone," Zack explained. "We have to get down there now to find out if somebody saw something."

"Zack's right, sweetie," Slater said to Jessie. "We have to try to get a description of these guys, at least."

Jessie nodded. "You're right."

"Does anyone remember what Kelly was wearing today?" Zack asked. "I think it was navy shorts and some kind of top."

"I thought she was wearing a skirt," Slater said.

"I don't remember," Jessie said, frowning. "Something pink?"

Lisa rolled her eyes. "She was wearing linen walking shorts in a shade of deep plum with a matching oversize blazer and a white tank top with an edging of pale green along the seams. No socks. White canvas shoes and a matching purse."

"I guess fashion can come in handy sometimes after all," Jessie said. She almost smiled, but she was too worried.

"Speaking of fashion, don't you have to get back to that Duncan guy's studio, Lisa?" Slater asked. "We know this is your big day."

"Don't even say it," Lisa said. "You know I would never leave you guys now. We have to find Kelly! I don't care about the show. Come on."

Zack, Slater, Lisa, and Screech headed for the door.

"Good luck!" Jessie called after them.

As soon as they were outside the hotel, they ran across the street to the square. Armed with an exact description of what Kelly was wearing, they made their way around the square. They asked everyone in sight if they'd seen Kelly, describing her in detail. Finally, Zack and Slater met back at the statue at the west corner of the square.

"No luck," Slater said.

Screech came up, already shaking his head. "Nothing," he said. "It's like she disappeared into thin air."

"I found one guy that remembers her," Zack said. "He'd been checking her out, I guess. But he doesn't remember seeing her with anyone. He said she disappeared when he went to get an ice cream."

Just then, Lisa ran up. "I think I've found a clue," she said. "Well, a little one, at least. One guy remembers Kelly sitting on that bench over there. He saw a guy talking to her. And he was eating something. I went over, and I found this." Lisa held out a crumpled-up bag from a fast-food joint.

"Not much of a clue," Slater said.

"But it's something," Zack said. "It's more than

we had before. Good work, Lisa. That was a smart idea, to go back and look for garbage."

"I remember seeing that place," Screech said. "It's just a half block from here."

Almost running, the group headed for the take-out store. This could really lead somewhere! But disappointment thudded through them as they questioned each of the counterpeople in the shop. Nobody remembered Kelly.

The pretty blond teenager behind the counter sighed. "It gets real busy during lunch," she said. "I wish we could help you, but we don't have time to breathe." She eyed Zack. "I *really* wish I could help you," she said.

Zack sighed. "Thanks, anyway."

Discouraged, they stopped outside the shop. "What should we do now?" Lisa asked.

"Go back to the hotel," Slater suggested. "Maybe Jessie's heard something by now."

With a savage flick of his wrist, Zack tossed the bag into the garbage. Anger pulsed through him, and he felt as though he were coming apart. He prayed that Kelly was safe. If only he could find her!

"Kelly, where are you?" he muttered through gritted teeth.

▲   ▼   ▲

"Where am I?" Kelly asked. Her voice sounded strangely high-pitched. She was scared. She couldn't see through the kerchief tied around her eyes. All she knew was that she was lying on the backseat of a moving car. "Who are you?" she asked.

"None of your business, princess," someone snarled. By the direction the voice came from, she figured that he was the driver. "And you don't need to know where you are, either."

"Why do I have to wear the blindfold?" Kelly asked. "I've already seen you, for heaven's sake. Some kidnappers."

"Hey," the other voice said, the one who Kelly thought of as the "nice" one, the one with curly red hair and freckles. Somehow, he'd looked familiar, and so had the other guy. "We're doing our best."

"You're making a big mistake," Kelly said, trying to sound brave. "My family doesn't have any money. I have six brothers and sisters, and my parents can barely keep us fed and clothed."

"We don't want your money," the driver snarled. "And shut up, will you?"

"Really," the redheaded one said. Kelly thought that he was really just trying to sound mean. He didn't have the same authority as the dark-haired driver. And to think she'd thought the driver was cute when he'd approached her in Union Square! He had the cutest crooked grin and twinkling blue eyes. He'd begged for her help—said his brother had lost the brand-new puppy they'd just bought for their sister, who was in the hospital. Would Kelly help them look for it? She couldn't believe that she'd fallen for such a dumb story. She'd followed them down to the underground parking garage, and before she knew what was happening, a gag was in her mouth and she'd been pushed into the backseat of a car! At least they'd taken off the gag after a while.

"You haven't stopped talking since we left San Francisco," the red-haired one complained.

"Hey!" the driver said, and Kelly heard the sound of a smack, as though he'd slapped the other guy on the leg. "That was real smart. We're not supposed to say anything about our destination, remember?"

"Sorry, Josh," the red-haired guy said contritely.

The sound of another smack resounded through the car. "No names, either!" the driver exploded. "For heaven's sake, Pete!"

"Hah! Got you!"

"I don't want to be critical or anything," Kelly piped up. "But you guys haven't done this before, have you?"

"How can you tell?" Pete, the red-haired guy asked.

"For starters, you kidnapped a poor person," Kelly said.

"We told you, we don't want money," Josh, the driver, said.

"Then what do you want?" Kelly asked. "And can't I sit up? I'm getting carsick."

"Ewwww," Pete said.

"Shut up, Pete," Josh said fiercely. "Don't listen to her."

Suddenly, Kelly smelled salt. They must be near the ocean. She felt winds shake the car. Maybe she was on the Golden Gate Bridge! It was supposed to be a very windy spot. Plus, it had definitely gotten colder. This morning, they'd seen fog obscuring the bridge, even though it was sunny downtown. Maybe they were taking her someplace in Marin County. Kelly hoped they weren't going far. Suddenly, a pang of fear shot through her.

Then suddenly, Kelly remembered where she'd seen the kidnappers. It was in Sausalito, the day before! They were the guys on the houseboat!

"Hey," she said. "I remember you guys now. I saw you in Sausalito yesterday. What's going on? Why did you kidnap me?"

"We just wanted to be heard," Pete said.

"So get a megaphone and let me go," Kelly said.

"Ha, ha," Josh said sardonically. "Everything's a joke to you, princess, isn't it?"

"No," Kelly said. "I'm scared, so I made a joke. Sue me."

"Funny you should say that," Josh said. "We've

tried suing that company you work for. We've tried writing letters and we've tried protests. And they still won't listen."

"What company?" Kelly asked, confused. They couldn't be talking about Yogurt 4-U. She'd never even started working there.

Josh made an exasperated noise. "The company that makes the product you're kissing up to on every billboard in California," he said witheringly. "Piglet Pops."

"Just northern California," Kelly corrected. "And what's wrong with Piglet Pops? I mean, I personally think they're pretty gross, but people seem to like them."

"How about that, Pete," Josh said. "She doesn't even eat them. 'Yum, yum, yum,' huh? I can tell we have a person of real integrity on our hands."

"Hey, I didn't ask you to kidnap me," Kelly complained. "And it's bad enough that you did. You don't have to insult me, too. What do you have against Piglet Pops, anyway? Did you get sick on them once or something? And speaking of getting sick, can I sit up?"

"Piglet Pops have made my whole town sick," Josh said. "Pete and I come from Pork Barrel, Oregon, where the Piglet Pop factory is. They've dumped so much pollution in the Crystal River, we had a town meeting and considered changing its name to Sludge. Our cancer rates are the highest in the Pacific Northwest, but the company won't do a thing about it. They couldn't care less."

"That's awful," Kelly said in a small voice.

"Yeah, it's awful," Josh said. She felt the car swerve, like it was leaving the freeway. It headed down a curving road. "But what do you care? Somebody tells you to hold up a box of something, and you hold up a box. Somebody tells you to smile, and you smile. You have a pretty face, and you use it. You never stop to think about what you're endorsing. You never ask the company what their policies are. Why should you? You just take the money and run. You run straight to a luxury hotel and spend your time sightseeing. Why should you care if you're the princess of pollution? You're having a good time."

Josh sounded truly disgusted. Kelly was silent. She wanted to shout at him, to tell him he wasn't being fair. She wanted to tell him how hard she had to struggle to get money for college. She wanted to tell him that she hardly ever got to go on a vacation. She wanted to say that she cared about the environment, too. She wanted to say all those things, but she couldn't. Because deep in her heart, she knew that Josh was right.

Chapter 10

When the phone rang, Zack sprang for it. But he paused before he picked it up, his hand on the receiver, and looked at each stricken face. "Ready?" he asked.

They all nodded solemnly. Slater gave him a thumbs-up gesture, and Lisa tried a wobbly smile. Zack picked up the phone and heard the voice of one of Kelly's kidnappers.

"I hope that you've followed our instructions," the voice said. It sounded kind of young, Zack thought.

"We have," Zack said evenly. "We haven't notified the authorities. Where is Kelly? Is she all right? Let me talk to her."

"She's fine," the voice said. "Now, listen. We are the voice of the people of Pork Barrel."

"What?" Zack asked. "Did you say pork barrel?"

"Pork Barrel, Oregon," the voice said. "We've kidnapped the spokesperson for Piglet Pops so that we could be heard. Our town has been destroyed by their processing plant. We demand a meeting with the board of directors of Piglet Pops."

"Best of luck," Zack snapped. "Where do we come in? I don't know the board of directors."

"Don't be a wise guy," the voice said. "Remember, I've got your girlfriend."

A cold finger of fear slowly trailed up Zack's spine. "What do you want?" he asked quietly.

"I want you to arrange a meeting with the board. I want a guarantee of our safety, and a time and place for the meeting to be set up. I'll call back in one hour. That's it."

"Wait," Zack said. "I want to talk to Kelly. Let me talk—" But he heard a click, and he banged the phone down in frustration.

Quickly, he filled in the gang on what the kidnapper had said.

Jessie looked shocked. "Kelly has been kidnapped by environmental activists? That's terrible. I'm tearing up my Green Teens membership card."

"What did the guy sound like?" Slater asked.

"Did he sound scary?" Lisa prompted.

Zack thought a minute. "It was weird," he said. "He sounded kind of young. And there was this sound . . . a background noise. It sounded kind of familiar, but I don't know what it was."

"Traffic?" Lisa guessed.

Zack shook his head. "It was like a clanging—only softer. Or maybe a pinging—only louder."

"Well, keep trying to remember. Now, let's talk about what to do next," Jessie said crisply. "We've got to contact the board of Piglet Pops. I think a couple of us should go to the library and investigate the company, find out if the story is really true."

"Good idea," Zack said. "Why don't you and Screech do that, Jessie? You're good at research. Meanwhile, Slater and I will look up the company offices and head over there. We're good at talking our way in anywhere," he said with a ghost of a smile.

Jessie turned to Lisa. "What do you want to do?" she asked. "There really isn't much else we can accomplish. We'll understand if you want to head over to Izzy's. We'll keep you posted."

"But—," Lisa started.

"Lisa, I mean it," Jessie said. "I really do. You have a huge commitment to the show, and your whole future might be riding on it."

Lisa looked into Jessie's eyes, and she saw that her friend was being honest. Warmth spilled through her heart, even through her fear for Kelly. She knew how hard it was for Jessie to tell her to go. "Forget it, kiddo," she said softly. "I'm staying. I already called the studio and said there was an emergency and I couldn't make it. And besides," she said, turning to the rest of them, "I just remembered something."

"What?" Zack asked eagerly.

Lisa held up a hand. "It could be nothing. But did you know that there's an underground parking garage in Union Square? It would be the perfect place for the kidnappers to get ahold of Kelly, wouldn't it?"

"Lisa, you're a genius," Screech said.

Lisa nodded modestly. "So while you guys are researching and talking your way into corporate offices, I'll do what *I'm* good at—flirting. Maybe I can find out something from the parking lot attendants."

"Let's just hope we make some headway," Jessie said anxiously. "And that Kelly's okay!"

"If they harm a hair on her head, I'll kill them," Zack vowed grimly. If he'd felt anxious and scared before, now he was ready to explode. All his feelings of love for Kelly were gathered in a tight ball in his throat. He could barely swallow, barely move, but somehow he was moving, and talking, and thinking. He had to keep going, he had to save her.

"What if they have her in some sort of awful place?" Lisa said fearfully. "Maybe they have her locked in a closet without food or water."

"Lisa!" Jessie exclaimed.

"Sorry," Lisa said in a small voice. But she had only voiced what everyone else was thinking. Who knew what terrible danger Kelly was in with a band of cutthroat kidnappers holding her hostage?

▲   ▼   ▲

Kelly reached for another slice of homemade pizza. "This is delicious, Pete," she said. "I can't believe I can actually eat, but I can."

"You really like it?" Pete asked. His thin, freckled face flushed with pleasure. "I started the dough this morning. And I went out and got sun-dried tomatoes for the topping, too."

"Delicious," Kelly said, chewing.

Pete went to sit next to Kelly on the couch. "Actually, I'd like to be a chef someday," he confided. "I really like to cook. Do you think that's weird?"

"Not at all," Kelly said. "My dad's a great cook. And lots of great chefs are men. I think you should do what you love to do."

Josh spoke up from across the room. "Pete," he snarled, "if you could *tear* yourself away from Her Highness, you might start cleaning up the kitchen. We're going to be leaving here in a hurry."

"Sure, Josh," Pete said, standing up. "Sorry, Kelly."

"Stop apologizing to her!" Josh roared. "She's our *prisoner*!"

Ducking his head, Pete hurried off toward the kitchen of the houseboat. When the door had closed behind him, Kelly put down her slice of pizza and turned to Josh.

"You don't have to be so mean to him," she said. "He's just trying to be nice."

"This isn't a picnic in the park," Josh growled. "I'm tired of him hovering over you, bringing you a soda, offering you food, fetching a blanket—what does he think this is, anyway?"

"Kelly?" Pete yelled from the kitchen. "Do you want some dessert?"

"That's *enough*!" Josh roared.

"He's being *nice*, which is more than I can say for you," Kelly said in a low tone. She settled back on the couch and looked away. If it weren't for Josh, she wouldn't be scared at all. Pete almost reminded her of Screech, with his bumbling attempts to be sweet. But Josh was just plain surly. Too bad he was so cute. If only he would lighten up a little, she wouldn't be scared at all. She'd just be angry.

"You know," Kelly said, "this is a big day for my best friend. Her dress is going to be in a big fashion show, and I'm supposed to model it. All these press people and rich people are going to be there. You're ruining everything for Lisa."

"Boo-hoo," Josh said sardonically.

"If you really cared about your fellow man, you'd have some sympathy," Kelly flung out.

Josh tossed his shiny black hair off his forehead and leaned forward. "I care about my fellow man," he said. "I don't care about a bunch of silly twits who spend thousands of dollars on a dress. I've got more important things on my mind. I'm trying to save my family and my town."

"Your family?" Kelly asked hesitantly.

Josh settled back in his armchair. "Don't worry, princess. Nothing for you to get concerned about. My mother started the Save Pork Barrel Committee. She was protesting at the factory, trying to dam up a pipe that was flowing into the Crystal River, and some thugs hired by Piglet Pops manhandled her. She's in the hospital right now."

Kelly's hand flew to her mouth. "That's terrible," she said. "I had no idea that Piglet Pops was such a horrible company."

"That's the trouble, isn't it, princess?" Josh asked steadily.

Kelly looked down at her hands. "I wish you'd stop calling me that," she murmured.

Josh sighed. "My dad used to work for Piglet Pops, but they fired him. He's out of work. Pete's dad is a salmon fisherman whose business dried up because the spawning grounds got too polluted. His uncle loaned us this houseboat—he's away on a

trip. We thought we'd come to the city and try to
see the board, appeal to them directly to start working with the town instead of against it. We don't
want the factory to leave, just clean up its act."

"What happened?" Kelly asked.

"They wouldn't see us." Josh shrugged. "Then
we recognized you, and I came up with this plan."

"What makes you think my friends will do any
better with the board of directors?" Kelly asked
curiously.

Josh gave a twisted smile. "They won't. They'll
chicken out and go to the cops. They'll be too scared
to play this one on their own. So we'll get into the
media, and *that* way the board might be embarrassed enough to do something."

"But, Josh, what about you and Pete?" Kelly
asked. "You'll be arrested."

Josh's jaw set. "I don't care," he said.

Kelly was silent for a moment. "There's only one
flaw in your plan, Josh," she said finally. "There's
something you don't know."

"What's that, prin—" Josh stopped. "What?" he
asked in a softer tone.

Kelly looked straight into his dark blue eyes.
"You don't know my friends," she said.

▲   ▼   ▲

"I think it's time to start thinking about calling the police," Jessie said. "Or at least telling my dad."

"Not yet," Zack said, drumming his fingers nervously. "Let's at least wait for Lisa to get back."

They were back in the girls' hotel room, waiting for the kidnappers to call again. In another five minutes, it would be exactly an hour since their first call.

"We just have to be patient for a little while longer," Slater told Jessie, taking her hand.

"Who knows how desperate these guys are," Jessie said worriedly. "Screech and I found out that the PPC—that's the Piglet Pop Corporation—is bad news. They're on the list of the ten most environmentally *un*concerned companies in the whole country. And last week, some of their goons sent a woman protester to the hospital." Jessie shivered. "This is serious stuff," she said.

"They're mean guys," Screech agreed. "At this point, I'm losing track of who the villains are."

"Tell me about it," Slater said. "The PPC had goons at the corporate offices, too. Zack and I couldn't get above the first floor. We'll never get them to meet with the kidnappers."

"So what's our next move?" Jessie asked.

"I don't know," Zack confessed. "I just wish we had a clue where they might have taken Kelly."

Just then, the door opened, and Lisa walked in.

"Well, I found out something," she said. "I don't know how much help it will be. I had to wait until one of the guys came back from his lunch break. He remembers Kelly really well. She was with two guys. But she didn't seem scared, the attendant said."

"That's strange," Jessie murmured.

"She just kept calling out 'Pookie! Pookie!'"

"Pookie?" Zack asked.

Lisa nodded. "As though she was looking for a kitten or a puppy. Then they went to the back of the garage. The funny thing is, the attendant said that when the guys drove out, it was only the two of them in the car."

"Maybe Kelly was in the trunk," Zack said.

Jessie gulped. "That's awful. We have to call the police, Zack." She stood up, twisting her hands anxiously. "We've got to!"

The sound of the phone made them jump. Zack snatched it up.

"What?" he barked.

"Testy, testy," the voice said. "Did you do what I asked?"

"Yes," Zack said. "We couldn't get past the receptionist. The Piglet Pop Corporation is like Fort Knox, fella. You'd better just let Kelly go. We can't help you."

"I'm not letting her go," the voice snarled. "You're just going to have to do better."

"I'm not doing anything until I talk to her," Zack said grimly.

There was a pause, and then Kelly's voice came on. "Zack?" she asked. "Is that you?"

"Kelly!" Zack gripped the receiver and closed his eyes. Kelly's voice through the receiver sounded like the sweetest song he'd ever heard. "Are you okay?" he asked anxiously.

"I'm fine," Kelly assured him. "Don't worry about me. I'm snug and cozy, Zack. Not shaky at all."

"Kelly, we're going to find you," Zack said desperately. "We—"

"Dream on, buddy," the sinister voice said, coming back on the line. He must have snatched the receiver away from Kelly. "You'll never find her. And she won't be snug and cozy much longer if you don't do what I say. I'm giving you one more half hour. That's it."

The kidnapper hung up. Zack heard the harsh buzz of the dial tone in his ear. He slammed down the phone.

"What did they say?" Slater asked.

"Nothing new," Zack said numbly. "We have to arrange the meeting with the PPC or else. Kelly didn't sound too scared. At least we know she's okay."

Zack sank down on the edge of the bed, trying to concentrate. A bunch of different thoughts were buzzing around in his head, and he couldn't make sense of them. Something about what Kelly had said. And something about that background sound he'd heard again. . . . Something slapping against something else. And then Kelly's bright voice. *I'm snug and cozy. Not shaky at all.*

Suddenly, the realization flooded through his brain like a blinding flash of light. Everything was illuminated, and he could have jumped for joy. Zack sprang to his feet. "I know where Kelly is!" he cried. "The Sausalito marina!"

Chapter 11

Everyone moved at once. Lisa grabbed her purse, smacking Screech in the head as she flung it over her shoulder. Jessie jumped for her father's car keys and knocked heads with Slater, who was starting toward the door. And when Screech tried to put on his jacket, he got tangled up with Zack, and they both crashed to the floor.

"Whoa!" Zack said from the floor. "Hold it! We can't get hysterical." He stood up. "Now, first of all, how are we going to get there?"

Jessie held up the car keys. "I borrowed my dad's car to go to the library. We can drive."

"But we don't know how to get there," Zack pointed out.

"There's a map next door," Slater said. "I'll get it." He dashed out the door.

"Zack, how did you figure it all out?" Jessie asked as they moved out to the hall to wait for Slater.

"Two things," Zack explained. "The sound I heard was the slapping of lines against the masts on a sailboat, so I knew it had to be a marina. Then Kelly said something about being snug and cozy. That's exactly what she said about living on a houseboat in Sausalito. I think she was trying to tell me that that's where she is."

"Wow, that's some detective work," Lisa said admiringly.

"And you weren't even wearing my Sherlock Holmes hat," Screech pointed out.

Slater emerged from their room, closing the door behind him. "Let's go," he said. "I'll look at the map while you drive, Zack."

The route to Sausalito was easy to figure out. Zack was driving onto the Golden Gate Bridge and heading across the bay in less than fifteen minutes.

"What are we going to do when we get there?" Jessie asked.

"I've been thinking about that," Zack said. "When Kelly and I were looking at the houseboats, we bumped into two guys who recognized her from her ads. Maybe if they're around, they've seen her with the kidnappers. I think I can find their place again."

"It's worth a shot," Slater agreed, poring over

the map to figure out the best exit for the marina.

"I hope they saw something," Jessie said.

Zack zoomed off the exit and quickly navigated the twisting streets of the Sausalito hills. Within minutes, he was pulling into the marina parking lot. Everyone piled out of the car and ran toward the docks.

"This way," Zack said, heading down a dock past a familiar-looking houseboat. He quickly ran down the dock, looking around anxiously. Then he recognized the houseboat that the two guys had been sitting on. It was smaller than the others, with a small turret rising up from the structure at one end.

"Here it is," Zack said. He stepped off the dock onto the small deck and knocked on the door. Slater followed him, and Screech, Lisa, and Jessie watched anxiously from the dock.

Zack heard noisy movement inside the house. "Hello?" he called. "I just want to ask you some questions."

He heard a thump, then the sound of footsteps. The door opened an inch, and a red-haired guy peered at him. His mouth dropped open when he saw Zack. "W-what do you want?"

"Remember me?" Zack asked in a friendly way. "Uh—I guess not. I was here yesterday with the Piglet Pop princess, remember? She's got long dark hair and blue eyes."

"Never saw her," the guy said. "I don't remember."

"Sure you do," Zack said. "You saw her at the Cannery, too. She's my age, really pretty, and—"

"Don't know her. I'm busy," the guy said. "Gotta go now. Bye."

He slammed the door in Zack's face. Puzzled, Zack turned back to Slater.

"Nice guy," Slater said as they started back toward the dock.

"That was weird," Zack said. "He definitely knew who Kelly was. He saw her three times—at the wharf, on the ferry, and here. They were really staring at her, too."

Zack stared at Slater. Slater stared back.

"Are you thinking what I'm thinking?" Zack asked.

Slater nodded. "You bet."

"Let's go." Zack turned and vaulted over the rail of the houseboat. He started toward the door to knock again, but Slater put a hand on his arm.

"Let's not announce our presence," he advised in a low voice. "Let's just go in."

"You mean break down the door? What if it's not them?" Zack asked.

Slater shrugged. "We'll have to pay for a new door. One, two—"

On the count of three, Zack and Slater put their

shoulders to the door and pushed. The door banged open. Zack's heart was pounding as he ran inside. Where was the girl he loved? Locked up? Hungry, cold, scared out of her wits?

Zack ran down a short hallway. He could see a light shining from a room on the left, and he burst inside.

Kelly was sitting on the couch, a blanket over her knees. A half-eaten pizza sat on the coffee table. She was laughing along with the dark-haired boy while the redhead poured her some soda. "No, I really couldn't have another bite," she said. "I'm—"

Kelly's mouth dropped open when she saw Zack and Slater crowded together in the doorway. Then she giggled. "Hi, guys," she said. "I've been waiting for you to show up."

▲　▼　▲

Everyone calmed down after a few minutes. After Kelly had thrown herself in front of Josh so that Zack wouldn't kill him, after Lisa had screamed, after Slater had hung Pete on a hook on the back of the door, after Screech had tasted the pizza. Kelly had begged them all to listen to Josh and Pete's story, and the group had finally quieted down and paid attention while Josh told them everything.

"We weren't going to do anything to Kelly," Josh said at the end of his story. "Actually, we were planning to take her back to the hotel at five o'clock and let her go."

"You expect us to believe that?" Zack scoffed.

"I believe it," Kelly said quietly.

Zack still glared at Josh and Pete, but Jessie sighed. "I have to admit I was really shocked when I read up on the PP Corporation," she said. "You guys have had a tough time getting through to them."

"We still shouldn't have kidnapped Kelly," Pete said.

Josh sighed. "I know. It was wrong. But when my mom landed in the hospital, I just went crazy. It was so frustrating not being able to get through to the company. Nobody would listen to us at all. We were desperate. But that's no excuse—I feel really badly that we had you so worried about Kelly." He looked over at Kelly. "Now I know how special she is."

"She sure is," Zack growled.

"Well, Josh was right about one thing," Kelly said. "When I model, I should be more aware of the companies I'm representing. There's no excuse for what I did."

Kelly looked so glum that Jessie patted her gently. "Kelly, don't be so hard on yourself. You can't present a list of demands if you're a model. You'd never get any work."

Kelly gave her a shrewd look. "But you would find out about what kind of company you were representing, wouldn't you, Jess?"

Jessie hesitated, then nodded. "But that's me," she said quickly. She grinned at Kelly. "You know that you don't like that kind of homework."

"Well, I'm going to do some from now on," Kelly declared. "That's what Josh taught me."

Zack couldn't believe it. Kelly was actually *thanking* her kidnapper. And he didn't like the way Josh was looking at her, either. His feeling of relief was slowly being nudged by jealousy. *Here I was frantic with worry while Kelly was sitting here giggling over a pizza with Mr. Blue Eyes*, he thought.

Kelly must have sensed his mood, because she sidled over a bit and slipped her hand into his. "I knew you'd find me," she whispered. "Just thinking about that made me feel less scared."

With Kelly's hand in his, Zack felt better immediately. There was an admiring glow in her beautiful eyes, too. Maybe this thing with Josh was just his imagination.

Pete rubbed his hands together. "Anyone for dessert?" he asked. "I could whip up some cookies. I was planning to send some back with Kelly when we drove her to the hotel this afternoon."

"Hey, what time is it?" Lisa said suddenly.

"It's three fifteen," Josh said.

Lisa jumped up. "The fashion show! We could still make it!" She looked at Kelly. "Do you think you could still do it?" she asked hesitantly.

Kelly nodded. "You bet."

Jessie looked at Josh and Pete. "I wish we'd been able to help you," she said.

Kelly looked stricken. "I feel the same way," she said to Josh. "Here I am running off to model for a group of silly twits who spend thousands of dollars on a dress."

"What?" Lisa asked.

Kelly giggled. "That's what Josh said before."

"Those silly twits are the wives of corporate directors," Jessie said dryly to Josh. "You might want to think about that." Then she snapped her fingers. "That's it!" she cried. "There'll be press and media and rich society people at this show—all the people you want to reach," she said to Josh and Pete.

"But what can we do?" Josh asked, shrugging.

Lisa checked her watch. "Whatever it is, we'd better get moving. We're cutting it real close."

Jessie sprang to her feet. "Come on," she said to Josh and Pete. "We'll think of something on the way."

"We will?" Zack asked darkly. He wasn't as ready to forgive Josh as everybody else was.

"Of course we will," Jessie said with a grin, giving Zack a look. "Don't we have the best scammer in the business?"

No way, Zack was about to say. But Kelly looked at him, her eyes shining. "Do you really think you could think of something, Zack?"

And just like that, his heart melted into a puddle of goo. "Sure," Zack said helplessly. "I'll do my best."

▲   ▼   ▲

They made it to the show with just minutes to spare. Izzy was so busy he didn't have time to say more than a quick hello to Lisa, so she didn't know if he was furious at her or not. The coordinator of the show grabbed Kelly and hustled her into a corner, where Lisa helped her into her outfit and ran to get the right accessories for it.

The other models hurried and scurried and wriggled into their outfits, shouting for their shoes or their eyeliner pencils. Lisa straightened the satin collar of Kelly's off-the-shoulder velvet dress and handed her the earrings she'd picked out.

"I wonder how Zack and the others are doing," Kelly said as she dabbed on lip gloss.

"Just worry about yourself right now," Lisa advised. "You're next. Zack will come through."

"He always does," Kelly said.

"Kapowski!" the coordinator yelled. "You're up!"

Just then, Jessie ran into the dressing room. She was holding a basket with a napkin draped over it, and she handed it to Kelly. "Here you go," she whispered. "Good luck."

Kelly hurried to the side of the curtain where the models left to walk out on the runway. Lisa dashed over to the announcer and handed her a slip of paper with Kelly's revised introduction on it. Lisa had already scribbled out the new script.

Kelly heard the announcer say, "And now, the winner of the California Young Designer to Watch Award, Lisa Turtle of Palisades, California, presents one of her own designs, worn by the Piglet Pop princess herself, Kelly Kapowski!"

Kelly swept outside. The lights dazzled her eyes as she walked down the runway with a big smile. Her nerves were fluttering like a thousand butterflies in her stomach, but she couldn't blow this moment for Lisa. She kept her head high and smiled as flashbulbs went off and the audience *ooh*ed and *ahh*ed.

"Kelly is wearing a deep claret velvet off-the-shoulder creation. Notice the satin collar in the palest shade of pink and the matching tiny, satin-covered buttons running up the back."

Kelly turned to show the back of the dress, then

turned again. She lifted the napkin off the basket as the announcer said, "And the Piglet Pop princess has . . . some treats for you?" The announcer ended the sentence in a puzzled way. This was obviously not part of the program.

Kelly reached into the basket and began to toss little hot dogs in blankets to the crowd. Zack and the gang had already heated them up in Izzy's microwave and twisted them into cocktail napkins. There was a roar of delight from the crowd at this unexpected, wacky development, and people unwrapped them and either examined them in a puzzled way or popped them into their mouths. The press seemed to find them especially delicious. One beefy guy with a video camera shouted, "Over here, princess!" and Kelly tossed him another hors d'oeuvre.

"Where's the mustard?" someone shouted, and Kelly got a roar of laughter when she tossed a plastic packet at the man. Zack had thought of everything.

"What's next for you, princess?" one of the reporters asked.

This was the question Zack had told Kelly she would get. And she had her answer. Kelly smiled demurely.

"My resignation," she announced dramatically. "I'm tossing away my crown!" She held up a Piglet Pop. "I hope you all enjoyed your snack. But did you know that you were supporting a major polluter by eating one of these?"

Flashbulbs popped and cameras clicked as Kelly tossed the Piglet Pop to the floor and wiped her hands in a disdainful gesture. "The Piglet Pop Corporation is behind a major pollution scandal!" she cried in a ringing tone. "If you want to know more, see me after the show."

Kelly swept off the runway to wild applause. She almost ran into Izzy on her way backstage, and he grinned at her.

"Looks like you stole the show," he said.

"I hope you don't mind my giving that speech," Kelly said. "It was for a good cause."

"I don't mind a bit," Izzy said. "The more publicity, the better."

Lisa ran up to Kelly. "You were fantastic!" she said.

Jessie, Zack, Screech, Slater, Josh, and Pete hurried up as well.

"How'd I do?" Kelly asked them. "I was so nervous!"

"You were great," Josh said. "Let's hope that they want to hear more."

"I think they will," Zack said. "I was in the audience, and the reporters were all saying they wanted to talk to Kelly. Maybe you should go out there now."

"Shouldn't I change first?" Kelly asked.

"No way, girl," Lisa said. "If your picture is going to be in the paper, I want it to be in my dress!"

"Spoken like a true designer," Izzy said. Then he linked arms with Kelly and Lisa. "Come on, you two. Let's meet the press!"

The rest of the group followed Izzy, Kelly, and Lisa to the front of the runway, where the press was waiting to congratulate Izzy and interview him.

After Izzy had spoken a few words about his collection and how impressed he was with Lisa's design, he was glad to turn over the floor to Kelly. The reporters were enchanted with Kelly's sparkling blue eyes and her passionate telling of the story of Pork Barrel, Oregon.

Pencils flew, cameras whirred, and video cameras were trained on Kelly as she spoke about corporate responsibility and her decision to quit. Zack had never felt so proud of her. He could hardly wait for the interview to be over so that he could tell her how fantastic she was.

The interview ended, and the reporters asked if she would pose for a few more photographs. "Of course," Kelly said graciously. She looked over the reporters' heads and her eyes suddenly warmed. She smiled.

Zack followed Kelly's bright gaze. She was looking at Josh, and he was looking back at her with the same warm admiration. Zack felt a sinking feeling in his stomach as he watched them gaze into each other's eyes.

Pain knifed through him, and he turned away. He just couldn't believe it. When Kelly had been kidnapped, he'd thought if only he could see her again, he could make everything all right. But now it looked as though he'd rescued her only to lose her to her kidnapper!

Chapter 12

As Kelly smiled at Josh and Zack headed out of the room, Izzy turned to Lisa and the rest of the gang. "This has been some crazy afternoon," he said. "Not only did we show a successful collection and make Lisa a star, but we saved a little town in Oregon."

"Let's hope so," Jessie said.

Lisa smiled at Izzy. "Thank you," she said quietly.

"For what?" Izzy asked.

"For not being angry at me," Lisa said. "I'm sorry I didn't show up today."

He waved a hand. "It doesn't matter. The show was a success, and that's what's important. And I couldn't be very angry at you, Lisa, no matter what. You're too sweet. Not to mention talented. Speaking of which, have you told your friends about your decision?"

Decision? Lisa's heart sank down into her shoes. She'd completely forgotten that she'd told Izzy that she'd come and work for him!

Jessie, Slater, and Screech all looked at her quizzically. "What decision?" Jessie asked, frowning.

Lisa wanted to sink through the floor. Just when things were back to normal with her friends, Izzy had to bring this up! "Well . . . ," she started.

Izzy slung an arm around her shoulders. "Lisa is coming to work for me!" he announced proudly.

"What?" Jessie asked. "You mean you're going to drop out of school?"

"She can finish up here," Izzy said.

"But, Lisa, what about your parents?" Slater asked.

"I *knew* disaster would strike on this trip," Screech said mournfully.

Lisa looked fearfully at Jessie. She expected her hotheaded friend to explode, but Jessie only looked concerned.

Izzy looked around at their faces. "I think I just blew it," he said. "I, uh, have some stuff to take care of in my office. I'll see you later, Lisa."

As soon as Izzy had walked away, Lisa turned back to Jessie. "I know you must be really mad at me," she said.

Jessie touched her arm. "I'm not mad at you,

Lisa. I feel really badly about the other night. You were right—I didn't really listen to you, and I didn't take your interest in design very seriously. None of us did. I'm sorry about that, but I still don't know if this is the right way to begin your career."

"Actually, I've been having second thoughts," Lisa admitted. "The show today was great. And spending time at Izzy's was fantastic, too. But when Kelly disappeared and we worked together to find her, I realized something, too. I'm not ready to start my career yet. I want to be a student awhile longer. I want to hang out with my friends, be a teenager, and have fun. After all, I'll be working the rest of my life. Why rush things? And I never thought I'd say this," Lisa added with a grin, "but I'd miss school. There's still plenty of stuff I want to learn."

Jessie gave her a hug, and Slater patted her shoulder. "I think you're making the right decision," Jessie told her.

Slater looked over at Screech, who had sunk down to the ground and was now sitting on the carpet. "Hey, Screech, are you okay?"

Screech nodded. "It's the shock of almost losing Lisa. I thought I was going to faint. What I need is nourishment," he said, picking up a stray Piglet Pop from the floor.

"Don't you dare eat that," Jessie said with a laugh. "Let's all go out for an early dinner instead.

My dad told me about this great Mexican restaurant near the hotel."

"Sounds terrific," Lisa said. "But I have to do one thing. I have to tell Izzy I changed my mind. I don't know how I'll find the words."

"I'm sure he'll understand," Jessie said soothingly.

"We'll wait for you," Slater promised.

"I'll wait forever," Screech told her worshipfully. "All of a sudden, the world is a wonderful place, after all."

Lisa shook her head happily. "I never thought I'd say this, but I think I agree with you, Screech."

▲   ▼   ▲

Lisa slowly climbed the stairs to Izzy's office. She was never good when it came to telling people how she truly felt. She usually stammered and hemmed and hawed, and then later, in the privacy of her room, she'd want to kick herself when she thought of all the things she *should* have said.

She couldn't let that happen with Izzy! He'd been so important to her, and she wanted him to know how grateful she was. She wanted him to know that he was asking her to give up something that was just as important to her as becoming a

designer was. And she didn't want him to feel hurt
or angry. How could she say all those things? She
didn't think she could ever find all the right words.

Lisa paused on the landing. She reached her
hand inside her big purse and pulled out her journal. She flipped through the pages until she found
her entry from last night. There, she'd written everything that she'd wanted to say. How she'd finally found her vocation, how Izzy had inspired
her, how much she admired him. If only she could
just read it to him instead of struggling for words.

Lisa climbed the rest of the stairs and knocked on
Izzy's office door. "Come on in," he yelled.

Lisa pushed open the door. "Hi," she said.

Izzy was standing at the drawing table, leafing
through some sketches. "Hi. How did it go with
your friends? I'm sorry I blurted it out like that."

"It's okay," Lisa said, coming forward into the
room.

Izzy put down the sketches he was holding.
"They didn't seem too thrilled about your coming
to work for me," he observed.

"They think I should stay in school," Lisa told
him.

He watched her warily with his soft, dark eyes.
"And what do you think?"

"I think they might be right," Lisa admitted
softly. She held out her journal, which was opened
to the entry from last night. "Izzy, I want you to

read this. You'll know exactly how I feel. Maybe I don't have the 'courage to be fabulous.' But I just can't drop out of school. No matter how I feel about you." She handed the book to him.

Izzy looked down. His face flushed a dark, angry red. Lisa's heart began to pound. Izzy was really angry at her!

He closed the book and stared down at it for a long time without saying anything. Finally, Lisa had to break the silence.

"Izzy, I know you're angry," she said. "But can't you read it?"

Slowly, he shook his head. He handed the book back to her. "No," he said. "I can't."

"But I want you to know how I feel!" Lisa said desperately.

Then Izzy finally looked at her, and there was pain in his eyes. "I didn't say I *won't*, Lisa. I said I *can't*."

Lisa felt as though her breath had been knocked out of her. "You mean . . ."

Izzy turned away and looked out the window. "I'm illiterate," he said quietly. "I told you that I dropped out of school when I was a teenager. I got through eleven years of school without learning how to read. It was hard, but I got good at faking it. I'm still good at faking it."

"You mean, like making your assistants read your mail to you while you work?" Lisa guessed.

Izzy turned back to her. He smiled a thin smile. "Exactly," he said. "Nobody knows, Lisa. Nobody knows but you. Even my closest friends don't know. I'm just too ashamed to tell them."

There was a long pause. Lisa didn't know what to say. She clutched her journal. "If you *had* read this, you'd know that I'm not good at talking about my feelings," she said haltingly. "That's why I write in a journal. And you'd also know that meeting you has changed my life. I didn't believe in myself before I met you, Izzy. I didn't really believe I had talent. You were the very first person to believe in me, to show me that talent is something that you should nourish, not throw away. It was the best gift I've ever gotten," Lisa concluded softly. "You're a great talent, Izzy. But you're generous, too. I'll always be grateful for what you've given me. And I'm sorry I can't do what you want."

Izzy shook his head. "I wasn't so generous, Lisa," he said. "I was selfish. I was trying to sell you on the idea that school wasn't important because I *wanted* to believe it was true. That wasn't a very nice thing to do. All my talk about having the courage to be fabulous is a joke. I'm the biggest coward of them all."

"No, you're not, Izzy," Lisa said. "You're still fabulous in my book. Even if you can't read it," she added with a grin.

Izzy flashed the smile that had made her go weak

in the knees from the very beginning. But his dark eyes still looked sad.

"Izzy," Lisa said hesitantly, "I don't want to butt in—"

"Since when?" Izzy asked, his eyes twinkling.

Lisa grinned. "Okay. So I'll butt in. Maybe it's time you did something about your problem. They have special programs, you know. Nobody has to know but you. It's better than living in fear, isn't it?"

He nodded slowly. "I've already decided it's time," he told Lisa. "Partly because of you. I spent so much energy convincing you that school isn't important that I realized how very important it really is."

"Oh, Izzy," Lisa sighed. "I'm really going to miss you." She knew now that her crush had just as much to do with Izzy's talent as with Izzy. It was more like hero worship than love. But it was still very special.

"You'd better stay in touch," Izzy said.

"I'll write," Lisa said.

Slowly, Izzy began to smile. "I'd like that," he said softly. "Just keep it pretty simple in the beginning."

"Are you kidding?" Lisa teased. "If I know you, you'll be reading *War and Peace* by next week."

Izzy laughed. "I don't know about that. But I know I'll be reading your letters."

"You'd better write me back," Lisa warned. "In between reading Tolstoy, that is. Promise?"

Izzy reached over and hugged her. "It's a promise," he said.

▲   ▼   ▲

"I'll write you," Kelly said.

Josh nodded. "I'll write you back," he promised.

Zack wanted to scream. He'd come outside for privacy, and he'd wound up overhearing Kelly saying good-bye to Josh! They were even holding hands. Zack pushed off the wall he'd been leaning against and crept away. His heart was already broken. He didn't need to get it stomped into little tiny bits, too.

He headed across the parking lot toward the bay. There was an old pier jutting out into the water, and he went all the way to the end of it. The cool breeze ruffled his hair, and he stared broodingly out at the distant Oakland hills. Maybe Screech was right, after all. Disaster *did* lurk around every corner.

Soft footsteps came behind him, and he was surprised when Kelly drew up by his elbow. She stared out at the bay, too. "Jessie sent me to find you," she said. "We're all going out for Mexican food."

"Sounds great," Zack said tonelessly. "Is Josh coming?"

"He and Pete are heading back to Pork Barrel tonight," Kelly said. "He wants to see his mother."

"Oh," Zack said.

"The whole experience was so weird," Kelly said wonderingly. "I mean, these guys kidnapped me. I should hate them. But I was never really very scared. And Josh taught me something important about myself, so I wound up being grateful to him."

"Totally weird," Zack said sourly.

"I think he's going to turn out to be a good friend," Kelly said softly.

Zack cleared his throat. He squinted across the bay until his eyes hurt. "Just a friend?" he asked casually.

"Yes, Zack," Kelly said. "Just a friend."

Something in her voice gave him hope, but he was afraid to trust it. Zack considered his options. He had to find out if there was a chance for him. After what he'd been through, he'd have a breakdown if he didn't. But what was the best way to find out? He'd have to rummage in his bag of tricks. Should he think of a new scam to get her to admit how she felt? Should he tease her, snow her, flirt with her, make her jealous, pretend he didn't care?

Zack turned to face her. Kelly looked at him quizzically. "Zack?" she said hesitantly.

Time is so precious, he thought. *And so is Kelly.* That was one thing Josh had taught *him.*

And sometimes, even the guy with all the answers could be at a loss for words.

"Zack?"

There was only one thing to do. He took the girl he loved in his arms and kissed her. His lips met hers gently, and Kelly gave a little sigh. Her arms slipped around him, and she returned his kiss with every ounce of the sweetness he remembered, and more. And Zack knew that he'd done the right thing at last.